"Don't offer me something you're not willing to give."

Peter knew his grin was inappropriate. But to see Thea so resolute, to hear the determination in her voice, surprised and pleased him. What could she possibly ask for that he wouldn't be willing to give?

"If you want me to stay and keep you company, Thea, all you have to do is say so. We can play cards, or you can show me how to sketch. There's no reason for you to be alone tonight if you don't want to be."

Her eyes narrowed, but he saw the way her hand trembled before she gathered a fistful of comforter into a tight ball within her palm.

"I don't want to be alone, Peter, but…"

"Fine," he said, wanting her to know she could ask him anything, trust him with her feelings. "I'll stay and we'll—"

"*But…*" She interrupted his reassurance, made his heart beat a little faster with the sudden fire in her dark eyes. "If you stay, we're not playing cards or…or anything like that." Her voice quivered. "Peter, I want…I want a…a wedding night."

Dear Reader,

Once again, Harlequin American Romance has got an irresistible month of reading coming your way.

Our in-line continuity series THE CARRADIGNES: AMERICAN ROYALTY continues with Kara Lennox's *The Unlawfully Wedded Princess*. Media chaos erupted when Princess Amelia Carradigne's secret in-name-only marriage was revealed. Now her handsome husband has returned to claim his virgin bride. Talk about a scandal of royal proportions! Watch for more royals next month.

For fans of Judy Christenberry's BRIDES FOR BROTHERS series, we bring you *Randall Riches*, in which champion bull rider Rich Randall meets a sassy diner waitress whose resistance to his charms has him eager to change her mind. Next, Karen Toller Whittenburg checks in with *The Blacksheep's Arranged Marriage,* part of her BILLION-DOLLAR BRADDOCKS series. This is a sexy marriage-of-convenience story you won't want to miss. Finish the month with *Two Little Secrets* by Linda Randall Wisdom, a delightful story featuring a single-dad hero with twin surprises.

This month, and every month, come home to Harlequin American Romance—and enjoy!

Best,

Melissa Jeglinski
Associate Senior Editor
Harlequin American Romance

THE BLACKSHEEP'S
ARRANGED MARRIAGE
Karen Toller Whittenburg

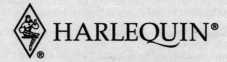

TORONTO • NEW YORK • LONDON
AMSTERDAM • PARIS • SYDNEY • HAMBURG
STOCKHOLM • ATHENS • TOKYO • MILAN • MADRID
PRAGUE • WARSAW • BUDAPEST • AUCKLAND

To Paula and Genell,
for lending me the courage to be brave

and

For Alitza,
whose enthusiasm has made writing
"The Braddocks" such a delightful experience.

ISBN 0-373-16919-1

THE BLACKSHEEP'S ARRANGED MARRIAGE

Copyright © 2002 by Karen Toller Crane.

Visit us at www.eHarlequin.com

Printed in U.S.A.

ABOUT THE AUTHOR

Karen Toller Whittenburg is a native Oklahoman who fell in love with books the moment she learned to read and has been addicted to the written word ever since. She wrote stories as a child, but it wasn't until she discovered romance fiction that she felt compelled to write, fascinated by the chance to explore the positive power of love in people's lives. She grew up in Sand Springs (an historic town on the Arkansas River), attended Oklahoma State University and now lives in Tulsa with her husband, a professional photographer.

Books by Karen Toller Whittenburg

HARLEQUIN AMERICAN ROMANCE

*The Magic Wedding Dress
†Billion-Dollar Braddocks

BRADDOCK FAMILY TREE

Archer Braddock m. Jane (d)

James Braddock

m.
..........Lily Hamilton (d)

Adam Braddock ①

Mariah Dellin (*)

Bryce Braddock ②

Catherine Latiker

Peter Braddock ③

(d) deceased
* affair
— — divorced
..... married

① *The C.E.O.'s Unplanned Proposal* 2/02
② *The Playboy's Office Romance* 3/02
③ *The Blacksheep's Arranged Marriage* 4/02

Prologue

Archer Braddock had attended many a wedding over the course of his lifetime, but none that pleased him more than this one. His Prince Charming of a grandson had finally met his Sleeping Beauty and today—this moment, in fact—they were facing each other in the First Methodist Church of Sea Change, Rhode Island, exchanging vows Archer had thought he might never live long enough to witness.

"Will you, Bryce Archer Braddock, take Lara Danielle Richmond to be your wife? Will you love her, honor her, comfort and keep her, keeping yourself only unto her for as long as you both shall live?"

And Bryce's voice rang out, confident and true, in the holy place. "I will."

It seemed only yesterday that Archer had stood in this same church, in front of family and friends, promising to love and honor his beloved Janey. But it had been more than fifty-four years since that day. Good years that had flown by in the blink of an eye. And today he sat alone, widowed, clutching the cherrywood cane that had been a gift from his dear wife and blinking back a mist of memories.

Beside him, his only son, James, sat still as a statue. Perhaps he, too, was pondering the marriage vows and examining his own experiences with them. Archer had only ever been married once. James had made and broken wedding promises many more times than that. It troubled a father's heart to see his son still grasping for an elusive happily ever after. Especially now that James's two oldest sons, Adam and Bryce, had found love and the perfect match for their proud hearts.

Standing on either side of Bryce and Lara, Adam and Katie, as best man and matron of honor, shared smiles and private glances, their eyes bright with happiness and the adventures they'd already shared in the three months they'd been married. No announcement had been made as yet, but Archer thought their excited whisperings and happy glow might mean he would be a great-grandfather before another summer rolled around.

Of course, Lara's four-year-old nephew, Calvin, had already bestowed that title upon him—called him "Grrranbad," which was Cal's abbreviated version of "Great Grandad Braddock." Already Archer loved his new nickname and the newest addition to the family. He loved the laughter and joy this one small boy had brought into Braddock Hall, and into these twilight years of his life. And in a few months, when Lara and Bryce completed their adoption of Cal, it would be official. Archer would, at long last, have a great-grandson. He wasn't sure how James felt about suddenly becoming a grandfather, but for his part, Archer was tickled right down to his seventy-nine-year-old toes.

At this minute, in fact, he was getting almost as much enjoyment out of watching Cal restlessly toss the ringbearer's pillow up and down, as he was in watching Bryce and Lara share their first kiss as man and wife. If only Janey could have been here with him, Archer would have deemed this the happiest day of his life. Of course, he'd thought the day Adam married Katie was the best. But now, to have a second grandson wed in the same year...well, life just kept getting better, that was all there was to it. So much good fortune in one lifetime. Archer was unspeakably grateful for all his blessings and more confident than ever that some things were simply meant to be.

Like he and Janey.

Like Adam and Katie.

Like Bryce and Lara.

Like Peter and the as yet unidentified young lady who was somewhere out in the world awaiting her knight in shining armor.

Archer feared this last Braddock match might be the most difficult of the three. Peter had come into the Braddock family circle late and, there was no doubt, he'd brought some heavy emotional baggage with him. Despite the whole family's best efforts to make him feel wanted and included, Peter hadn't seemed to feel he belonged, had never seemed to think he quite *fit* in the midst of the Braddock family. Even now, at twenty-seven, he acted at times as if he believed he still had something to prove, as if there were some test of honor he was required to pass before he could lay a legitimate claim to the history and honor of the Braddock name.

Archer only hoped Ilsa Fairchild could work one more miracle and find the right woman for Peter. Someone who could, perhaps, soften the rough edges of his prodigal heart and help him believe he was, indeed, a fine and worthy young man. It didn't seem likely any of the lovely debutantes he usually preferred had that kind of patience, but if there was one out there, Archer knew Ilsa Fairchild would find her.

He knew now it had not been a mistake to engage a professional matchmaker of uncommon perception, high ideals and an amazing record of success stories. Having heard discreet whispers about her abilities, he'd approached Ilsa, calling himself all kinds of an old fool for believing she could help his grandsons find their own true loves. But she'd taken on the task with her usual ladylike flair and produced two surprising, but delightful, matches. Now only Peter remained.

And James.

Archer knew better than to mention his son to Ilsa as a potential client. She claimed all she did was study, observe and assist a truly seeking heart, but that it wasn't in her power to work miracles. James, who was perpetually engaged to one unsuitable younger woman or another, didn't require the services of a matchmaker, in Ilsa's stated opinion, so much as he needed a good therapist.

But Archer loved his son and he knew, in his heart of hearts, that what James needed and wanted most, was the love and respect of a woman like Ilsa. And there were signs even an old man couldn't miss. Ilsa's interest in James, James's interest in Ilsa, despite how hard each of them tried to disguise the attraction. Archer wasn't blind to his son's flaws, but he didn't believe James was beyond redemption, either. Far from it. And as a father, Archer wasn't above introducing a few matchmaking *possibilities* himself. Just because James was a fool about women didn't mean he wouldn't recognize the real thing when it was right in front of his nose, and Archer intended to make every effort to place Ilsa right in front of James's nose as often as possible.

After all, he'd watched Ilsa work her discreet and delightful magic on both Adam and Bryce and he'd learned to recognize a good *possibility* when he saw one. Ilsa and James were a good match. All they needed was the opportunity to recognize that for themselves.

Music purled through the sanctuary as Bryce and Lara came down the aisle, all smiles, as husband and wife. *"Ah, Janey..."* Archer sent the thought winging heavenward, sharing this precious, long-awaited moment with his dearest wife and friend. *"It's a good day for the Braddocks. A very good day."*

ILSA FAIRCHILD kept her eye on Theadosia Berenson throughout the wedding reception at Braddock Hall. Not a particularly difficult task, since Thea had left the periphery of the outdoor party only twice so far this evening, both times to fetch a drink for her grandmother. What hold did old Davinia Carey have over her granddaughter? Ilsa wondered. And why did Thea continue to live on at Grace Place with her grandmother, when she was over twenty-one and possessed a sizeable fortune of her own? It was a strange relationship and it bothered Ilsa a great deal, mostly because of a persistent, niggling impulse to set up an *introduction of possibilities* between Thea and Peter Braddock.

Such a match would never work, would never even get past the initial setup. Not in a million years. But something drew her thoughts to Thea every time she set her mind to finding a love match for Peter. She was losing her touch, obviously. And Ilsa did not enjoy the feeling. Not that every match she set up worked out. Not that she believed every possibility would result in a fairy-tale ending. Life wasn't that orderly and sometimes what might have been the perfect match under one set of circumstances, turned out to be entirely wrong under another set. But this time her instincts seemed to be leading her in a completely wrong direction right from the start, and that hadn't happened before. Ever.

Certainly the Braddock men had been her biggest challenges in years. They were all handsome, all intelligent, all wonderful young men, heirs of a proud and prosperous New England family. They were gentlemen, born and reared, possessed of the same old-world manners and charm as their grandfather and their father. Adam had been a relatively easy match—almost anyone could have seen the sparks of attraction that flew between Katie and Adam the minute they met. It had taken only a little ingenuity and a bit of luck to set their hearts onto the same path. With Bryce, it had taken longer, required some serious study, but the tension that sizzled in the air between he and Lara was unmistakable. Once Ilsa recognized it and realized their hearts had already chosen each other, it was relatively easy to bring their possibilities into focus.

But Peter was different, tougher in ways Ilsa couldn't quite divine. And her intuition, which rarely led her astray, kept turning her in the direction of Thea Berenson, the definitive ugly duckling.

Maybe it was time to take on an apprentice. Training someone in the intuitive arts might help Ilsa refocus her own abilities, sharpen her perspective, and—if nothing else—at least, give her someone with whom she could discuss ideas. Since Adam's marriage to Katie, business at IF Enterprises had increased markedly, and just since the announcement of Bryce's engagement, she'd had private referrals from as far away as South Carolina. Not that she intended to advertise or expand her business outside of New England, but perhaps it was time to think about the future and a time when she might not find matchmaking such a delightful endeavor.

"No frowning now, Ilsa." Archer came up behind her and steadied himself with his cane. A handsome man for all of his seventy-nine years, Archer had become her friend during these past months as the two of them had talked, planned and hoped to find a match for each of his three grandsons. "Not when Bryce and Lara are so happy. Not on their wedding day."

"Who could frown while watching Calvin? He's having a perfectly grand time, isn't he?" She offered the smile he'd requested with hardly any effort at all. "A bonus for you, Archer. A great-grandson, as well as another lovely daughter-in-law."

"A bonus, indeed," Archer agreed. "But Janey is whispering to me right now that you're the one who deserves a bonus." He pulled an envelope from his inside coat pocket and extended it to her. "You've more than earned it, Ilsa."

She looked at the envelope. "A lovely gesture, Archer, but I can't accept that. I've only done what you hired me to do, and my fees are the only compensation necessary. Besides, there's still Peter left."

"Yes, yes." Archer looked toward the dance floor, where his grandson was dancing with a willowy blonde, under a canopy of tall trees, discreet lighting and a starlit sky. "There's still Peter." He turned again to Ilsa, his smile gentle with the pleasures of a long life well spent. "I know I'm not supposed to ask, but any prospects for him as yet?"

"I've had a thought, but…" She shook her head. "No, I don't think it's right. He'd never get past who she is."

Archer watched the dancers in silence for a moment or two. "Peter does have a fascination with the debutantes. The bluer the blood, the better he seems to like them. I'm afraid trying to work one of your *introduction of possibilities* with someone outside of that inner circle may prove difficult." His lips curved with a very gentlemanly smile. "Of course, you've already proven yourself to be a miracle worker, Ilsa."

"I'm having serious doubts about my ability this time." She paused, hating to ask, but needing to know. "Can you tell me something about Peter's life before he came to live with you, Archer? Not now, but perhaps we can have lunch one day soon and you can give me a little better understanding of him."

With a soft sigh, Archer inclined his head. "Of course. That would, I think, shed some light on the man he is now. I will tell you that we didn't even know Peter was in the world until he was nine. By that time, his mother had told him so many different things about this family, I honestly think he believed we were royalty or some such nonsense. If Janey hadn't immediately set about to demystify the family history to make him feel a part, I'm not sure Peter would ever have felt he belonged with us." Archer shifted his weight and brought his old eyes back to her. "I'm sure you know some of the story. We tried to keep the circumstances out of the newspapers, but it was quite a scandal at the time.''

"I heard some things," Ilsa said, because it was true. "But because I knew James, I always believed there was a great deal more to the story than the newspapers printed."

"James swears he never knew about the boy," Archer said, his gaze steady on hers. "Janey and I believed then...and now...he would have done something to prevent the tragedy had he known."

"James may be guilty of poor judgment when it comes to choosing a wife, but I know he genuinely loves his sons."

Archer's smile emerged with a touch of youthful glee. "I imagine you've noticed Monica's conspicuous absence today."

Ilsa didn't want to show too eager an interest in those details, although she was dying to know what had happened between James and his latest fiancée. "I did wonder where she was."

"Colorado," Archer said with satisfaction. "Day before yesterday, she left in a huff. At James's request."

A whisper of excitement stole through Ilsa for no good reason. "I'm surprised she didn't at least stay for the wedding."

Archer chuckled. "She would have if James hadn't been adamant about her leaving sooner rather than later."

"A lover's quarrel, perhaps?"

"More like an unholy war. He was unhappy with

her from the start and I never thought he'd go through with the marriage, anyway. But the important thing is, Ilsa, that James is no longer engaged to be married and I think this could be the perfect opportunity to make an *introduction of possibilities* for him."

That Archer had illusions of making a match between her and his son was no secret to Ilsa. What she hadn't bargained for was the unexpected thrill of anticipation she felt at the possibility. "I believe I've said this to you before, Archer, but matchmaking is not a precise science and does hold more than its fair share of disappointments."

He smiled, undaunted. "One of the wonderful things about being an old man, is that fear of disappointment isn't much of a determent. But there, I don't wish to embarrass you. I simply would like to give you this bonus check before I go out there and persuade my new granddaughter-in-law to shuffle once around the dance floor with me." He extended the envelope to Ilsa again with a look that asked her to take it without further protest.

"Keep the check, Archer," she said. "At least until we see if I can even come up with a suitable possibility of a match for Peter. At the moment, I'm beginning to doubt my own better judgment."

Archer regarded her for a moment, then tucked the envelope back into his jacket pocket. "As I occasionally have told my grandsons, 'Trust your instincts. God gave them to you for a reason.' Or as Janey put it so much more eloquently, 'Follow your impulse. You never know when one may turn out to be exactly, exquisitely right.' And now, Ilsa, my dear, if you'll excuse me, there's a beautiful bride, who is, I believe, saving a dance for me.''

Ilsa watched him, marveling at what a courtly appearance he made as he moved through the crowd, never asking for the space to maneuver with his cane, but rather commanding it by the simple measure of a smile here, a word of greeting there. Her glance turned again to Peter, dancing now with Thea Berenson. A duty dance. Anyone looking at the mismatched couple could see that. Peter was nothing if not a gentleman. And Thea was, to her core, a lady.

Follow your impulse.

She let the possibility float as she watched Thea look everywhere but at the man who was holding her at a respectful distance, doing his best to initiate some conversation. And having little success with it, too. Ilsa caught sight of James, moving through the crowd toward her. Stopping to chat along the way, but catching her eye to let her know she was his destination.

Her heart picked up a silly rhythm of anticipation and she tried to force her thoughts back to Peter and Thea. Thea and Peter.

But James came closer and she began to smile without having any intention of doing so. For the moment, at least, she'd just have to set aside her reservations about a match for Peter Braddock and concentrate all her energy on not falling victim to his father's considerable charm.

Chapter One

Peter tried on half a dozen shirts before he found the right one.

He didn't want to look too formal, because that might make her uncomfortable. He didn't want to look too casual, because that would make him uncomfortable. He didn't want to wear anything too plain and have her thinking he'd dressed down in an attempt to match her, because that could be awkward, as well. But finally, he buttoned up the green Armani silk shirt and grabbed the matching tie, looping it around his neck and tying it in a neat Windsor as he trotted down the stairs, his jacket slung across his arm.

He did not want to be late for this date. No, sir.

What he *wanted* was to skip it altogether.

But he was descended from a long line of gentlemen and standing up a lady just wasn't anything a Braddock would ever do. Even if he wanted to. Even if his grandfather hadn't specifically asked him to do this one small favor for an old family friend. Peter couldn't see that Davinia Carey was anyone's friend, but that was beside the point. His grandfather had asked him, and Peter couldn't refuse—wouldn't even dream of refusing—this single, simple request.

So he would escort Theadosia Berenson—the nightmare date of all time—to Angela Merchant's wedding and pretend there was no place he'd rather be and no one else he'd rather have at his side.

It was a small enough price to pay for all the Braddock family had given him. A home, when he had nowhere else to go. A family, when the only one he'd known fell apart at the seams. A name to take pride in, when he was marked by shame and scandal. He owed everything to Archer and Jane Braddock. And to his father, James. They'd saved his life, made a man of him. And a gentleman, at that.

Which was the reason Thea would never know she wasn't his dream date for the evening.

He took the last two steps in one bouncy stride, loving the savvy click of his heels as they struck the marble floor.

"Peter?"

Slinging his jacket across his shoulder, he walked quickly to the door of the library, where Archer and James sat before a fire, the first of the season though—it seemed to Peter—more for ambiance than warmth, even now. An ivory chess set was on the table between them, the game clearly heating the normal father and son tensions. James had been at Braddock Hall for nearly five months now, longer than any of his sons could remember him staying in the past and, having recently broken his engagement, he was in the restless stage of being newly single again.

Peter recognized the signs, knew his father didn't miss Monica as much as he missed the idea of himself with the young and beautiful Monica. But it was a good thing the relationship had ended when it had. Peter didn't have any use for women like the ones his father invariably chose, and Monica had been the worst of the lot. So far.

"Where are you headed?" James asked, studying the chessboard before carelessly moving his pawn.

"To Newport. Angela Merchant's wedding is this afternoon at four." He smiled at his grandfather, proud to have been asked to perform this one small good deed. "I'm on my way to pick up my date."

Archer didn't smile back, looked slightly guilty even as he moved to block James's bishop.

"Which beautiful blonde are you taking to this wedding?" James frowned absently as he studied the chessboard and Archer's bid to check. "The lovely Lindsay? The delicate Daphne? The ethereal Emily?"

"Today," Peter said in his most courtly tones. "It's my privilege to be escorting Miss Thea Berenson."

James's frown turned dryly cynical. "Fine, don't tell me who you're taking."

"I'm escorting Thea," Peter repeated. "I'm picking her up at Grace Place and taking her to the wedding. As my date."

James looked up then, his eyes—so like Peter's own—narrowed suspiciously. "You *asked* Thea Berenson to be your date to Angela Merchant's wedding?'' he said incredulously. ''Is this your idea of a joke?''

''No, sir,'' Peter said, offended by the question, even though he knew most everyone would think what James was clearly thinking now. It was one thing to dance with someone like Thea at a social gathering. *That* was considered the mark of a gentleman. But to *ask* to escort an acknowledged wallflower to an event, to make it into an actual date, was another thing entirely. In the unwritten laws of chivalrous behavior, it was considered misleading, unkind and nothing a gentleman would ever do unless he had a genuine interest in the lady. Which, of course, Peter didn't. But Archer had made the request and Peter wasn't going to apologize to anyone for acceding to it. ''I not only asked,'' he told James with an easy smile, ''but was accepted. That's usually a prelude to a pleasant evening, as I fully expect this one to be.''

James looked at Peter thoughtfully, then his gaze swiveled to Archer. ''Is this *your* idea of a joke? Thea Berenson? Come on, Dad. You don't honestly think she and Peter could ever...''

''I honestly think Peter should go now before he's late,'' Archer said, with an upward glance that barely met Peter's eyes before skittering away. ''Davinia is a stickler about punctuality.''

Peter frowned, wondering at his grandfather's odd tone. Surely, Archer didn't believe Thea was that bad. She wasn't much to look at, true. She didn't have much to say for herself, either. And she wore clothes more suitable for a prim nineteenth century schoolmarm than a twenty-first century debutante. But Peter had never thought she was as hopeless as most people seemed to think. He'd certainly never thought of her as the ugly duckling some of his friends considered her to be.

Which didn't mean he was looking forward to the evening. Quite the contrary. But he didn't think it would be unbearable, either, as his father clearly did. And he didn't believe Thea had any misconceptions about his reason for asking her out. They were attending the event together because their grandparents had decided they should. End of story. "Grandfather's right. I should go. It wouldn't do for a Braddock to be late for a date...no matter who it is or what the circumstances."

"Peter," James said, his gaze narrowed firmly on Archer. "I think you ought to know that your grandfather has been engaging in some match—"

"—hopeful contemplation," Archer interrupted firmly, "that you and Miss Berenson will have a perfectly lovely evening. And that you will be, as you always are, a perfect gentleman."

"I believe you can safely count on that." Peter tossed the keys to his BMW roadster and caught them with confidence. "It's the one thing you can always count on your grandsons to be. Good night, Dad. Grandpop," he said. "I'll see you tomorrow at breakfast."

Peter turned and started out, then paused to flash a grin over his shoulder at James. "Oh, and Dad, watch out for your queen. Looks like Grandpop is just about to turn her into a damsel in distress.''

THEA CREPT ALONG THE tree limb, keeping a firm grip on the branch with one hand and pausing every few inches to scoot the down comforter bundled beneath her so she wouldn't scratch her bare thighs on the rough bark. She'd jerked the comforter from her bed without a thought as to how slippery it would be, just as she'd climbed out on this limb without stopping to consider that she was a wee bit underdressed for tree climbing. But it was too late for second thoughts at this point. She was several feet up in the old oak, straddling the down-filled comforter for all she was worth and wishing she had never rescued the calico kitten from an untimely end in the first place.

Ahead of her and one narrow branch above her head, the kitten yowled out a fearful screech of a sound. "Would you quit that, Ally?" Thea said softly. "If Grandmother finds us in this tree, it'll cost you at least eight of your nine lives, and you don't have that many left." It would mean a stern lecture for her, too, but Thea didn't imagine the kitten would care much about that. As dearly as she loved all of her pets, none of them seemed to appreciate the sacrifices she made in order to keep them in the manner to which they'd become accustomed.

Inching forward just a bit farther, she lifted a tentative hand up to the little calico, which fuzzed and arched her back in fright, before backing up another few inches along the tree limb.

"Come on, Ally. I'm here to help. Honest." She coaxed the kitten with low, soothing tones, as she hugged the comforter with her thighs and scrooched farther along the oak branch. "How many times do we have to go through this drill before you trust me to get you back inside?"

The kitten meowed plaintively, her tawny eyes rounded in distress, her claws clenched on the tree like tiny anchors. Thea calculated the distance from where she was to where the kitten was, and back to the attic window from where she'd started this rescue mission. Grace Place, her grandmother's childhood home, loomed large and sullen beside the leafy old oak, the open attic window the only inviting element in the otherwise hulking structure. But a home was more than stones and mortar. Grace Place was all the home Thea had ever known, her grandmother all she knew of family. The house really wasn't so bad. It had potential and someday, when her grandmother was no longer around to protest every change, Thea imagined it would look very different with gardens of bright flowers and shutters painted a soft cream, instead of stark black. Inside the house, she'd replace the heavy draperies with open-weave curtains, which would welcome every drop of sun, warming the rooms with natural light, instead of conserving every degree of artificial heat within by keeping the outside weather out.

But someday wasn't today.

Today was Angela Merchant's wedding day and, if Thea didn't get this silly kitten out of the tree, get herself inside and dressed, she was going to miss one of the biggest social events of the season. Not that she'd mind in the least. But her grandmother wouldn't hear of such a thing, which meant Thea was going to the wedding, by gum or by golly.

If only Davinia hadn't decided that this time Thea required an escort....

Like a bad omen, she heard the distant throb of a powerful engine and her heart picked up the throaty rhythm, adding in a ragged, anxious beat. Peter Braddock was on his way to get her. By the sound of it, he was nearly at the gate, which meant he'd be ringing the front bell in ten minutes. Or less.

She entertained a fleeting thought of staying up in the tree and hoping no one would find her. But that was merely wishful thinking. Monroe always found her, no matter how well she thought she was hidden. Thea frowned meaningfully at the kitten. "This is it, alley cat. Either you come with me now, or you'll have to get yourself down. What's it to be?"

She extended her arm as far as possible and coaxed in low, persuasive tones, "Here, kitty, kitty. Come on, kitty...."

The calico seemed to sense her last chance and, crouching low on the limb, made a tentative move toward Thea's outstretched fingers. "That's right," Thea coached. "Just a little bit farther..."

The low purring of the sports car's engine slowed,

indicating it had reached the gate. Peter was probably buzzing in even now and once the gates swung open, it wouldn't take him two minutes to reach the house. Thea knew it was now or never, so she made a grab for the cat. Catching hold of one furry leg, the whole scrabbling, scratching ball of fur came tumbling into her arms and tried to climb her shoulder. "Stop it, Ally," she said, trying desperately to calm the kitten and maintain her grip on the tree branch. But her balance was off and the down comforter was slip-sliding dangerously. All Thea could do was hold on to the cat as she tipped to the side and fell, shielding the kitten with a last-minute hunching of her shoulders.

She hit the ground in a rolling thud, thankfully cushioned by the soft bulk of the down comforter, and clambered to her feet, still holding on to the kitten and ignoring the sharp ache in her hip. The engine had revved again, preparatory to sweeping around the curving drive to the house, and she knew her window of opportunity was fading fast. If she didn't get in the house immediately, Peter Braddock was going to drive up and see his date for the evening clad only in her silk slip. Leaving the comforter pooled at the base of the tree, Thea made a wild, limping dash for the back of the house, praying fervently that Monroe had left the door to the servants' quarters unlocked and that Peter Braddock would turn out to be extremely nearsighted.

PETER CAUGHT A GLIMPSE of a scantily clad female form—a rather nice form from what he could see—

running around the corner of the house as he drove up. Funny. He'd heard that the only females at Grace Place were old Davinia, Thea and the elderly retainer's plump wife. Apparently, though, there was at least one slim, young and attractive woman on the household staff. Either that, or one of the groundskeepers had invited his girlfriend over for a little afternoon delight. Wouldn't Mrs. Carey have a fit if she knew about that? She'd probably string the man up by his thumbs and post him by the front gates as a warning to anyone else with lascivious appetites who might step foot on her property. Thea's grandmother seemed a regular tyrant, a throwback to another era, an idealist who believed the restraints and restrictions of Victorian England still had a place in twenty-first century America.

Peter turned off the engine of the car, pocketing the keys as he stepped out onto the paved drive. He'd always felt a deal of sympathy for Thea, caught in a life she surely wouldn't have chosen for herself. There were rumors about Thea's mother, Davinia's willful and rebellious daughter. Peter didn't know if the rumors were true or if, in fact, they had anything to do with the tight rein Davinia held on her only surviving grandchild. He didn't have a clue as to why Thea allowed herself to be governed by her grandmother's outdated ideas and ideals. It wasn't as if she had no other recourse. Everyone knew she had considerable assets of her own.

Not that it mattered to him one way or another. He

had no intention of giving Thea or her grandmother any grounds for complaint. Not tonight or at any time in the future. He couldn't imagine even a single circumstance under which he'd be tempted to behave as anything other than a perfect gentleman with Thea. She wasn't exactly his idea of a temptress.

The idea of Thea as femme fatale made him smile as he loped up the steps and pushed the doorbell, half expecting to be admitted by a butler straight out of the old *Addams Family* television series. But the liveried man who opened the thick wooden door looked more like Santa Claus than Lurch. "May I help you?" the butler said.

"I'm Peter Braddock." Peter offered the information with a smile. "I believe Ms. Berenson is expecting me."

"Miss Thea isn't quite ready, sir, but Mrs. Carey would like to greet you in the parlor."

Disguising his reluctance to be *greeted,* Peter stepped inside the cavernous foyer and blinked in the dusky, dusty light. Grace Place, on first impression, did not live up to its name. Although as his vision adjusted to the gloom, he could see the house might once have been something spectacular. Dual stairways curved up on either side of a large entry and the chandelier hanging from the ceiling was quite simply massive. If lit it would undoubtedly illuminate the entryway with a crystalline light.

"This way, please." The butler walked with a slight hitch in his step to the far side of the foyer, where he opened an ornately carved wooden door to reveal a dim room decorated in a style that hadn't been fashionable for forty years. "Mr. Peter Braddock is here for Miss Thea," he announced, then stepped aside so that Peter could enter the parlor, which was just as dreary as the foyer, if not more so.

Davinia Carey sat like the proverbial spider, in a web of ruffled cushions on a dark green velvet settee. Her hair was crimped and upswept into a tight knot atop her head. It was as black as a raven's wing, which made her face look unnaturally pale in the gloomy light. "Good afternoon, Peter," she said in a voice that made him feel he wasn't standing quite straight enough.

Peter wasn't easily intimidated, but Davinia Carey always made him nervous, as if she was both judge and jury, as though she knew that beneath his *GQ* facade he was merely a pretender to the throne. "Hello, Mrs. Carey," he replied in a voice that betrayed not one iota of his feelings. "It's very nice to see you again. I hope you're feeling well today."

She sniffed, a sound as eloquent as any words. "Have a seat, Peter."

He glanced around and chose a straight-backed Queen Anne, which was as uncomfortable as it looked, but had the advantage of being a respectable distance from the settee. For some reason, he found himself remembering the night of his first formal dance. He'd been a gawky, awkward kid, barely thirteen, and still terrified he would do something to embarrass the whole

Braddock family. He'd made himself sick worrying about the dance and what he should or shouldn't say to the pretty girl who was his date, until Grandmother Jane had taken him aside and offered her wise counsel. *"Some day, Peter,"* she'd said. *"You'll meet the woman who will be your wife and you'll realize that her opinion of you truly matters. This is not that day, so stop worrying, relax and simply do your best to have a good time."*

Well, today was not that day, either. And with the thought, he offered Davinia Carey a warm and kindly smile. "I've never been to your home before," he said easily. "Grace Place is an impressive estate."

"It's nothing to what it was when I was Thea's age. This house is not as old as Braddock Hall, but my great-great-grandfather, Davis Madison Grace, spared no expense in building it."

Which didn't keep it from looking like a very poor relation now, Peter thought but didn't, of course, say aloud. "I believe Grandfather mentioned this was your childhood home."

The sniff again. This time expressing nostalgia, perhaps, or some old regret for days gone by. "My coming-out ball was as grand as any party ever given at The Breakers, I can assure you. Ask your grandfather. He'll remember." She paused, her eyes narrowing on him. "Grace Place will belong to Theadosia one day."

He didn't know quite how to respond to that, but she seemed to expect a reply, so he said, "Lucky Thea."

"Luck has nothing whatsoever to do with it, Peter. She was *born* an heiress."

The slight stress on the word was, he felt, not only intentional but intended to remind him that he *hadn't* inherited the Braddock name and its privileges at birth. He had, in fact, spent the first nine years of his life believing he was the son of another man, a poor man, and hadn't even been acknowledged as a Braddock until he was nine. A lot of people knew that. It wasn't exactly a secret. But no one had ever pointed it out to him in such a coldly calculating way. Davinia Grace Carey was telling him he was not good enough for her granddaughter and it was all Peter could do not to challenge her on it. As if Thea had suitors climbing the walls of this monstrous old house in the hope of winning her heart. Or at least her fortune.

He held the old woman's gaze and didn't politely look away when it grew uncomfortable. "As I said before, lucky Thea."

She drew herself up at that and a haughty smile curved along her thin lips, making her look even more like a spider in no particular hurry to immobilize her prey. "I see that we understand each other, Peter. I'm not sure what Archer had in mind in setting up this assignation between you and Thea. Do you know?"

Peter breathed deeply to maintain his composure. "I believe he hoped we would have a pleasant evening."

"Be that as it may, Thea has been brought up as a lady and I do expect you to treat her as such. You will have her home at a reasonable hour. Not a moment past midnight, and in the same virtuous condition as when she walks out the door with you.''

It was becoming very clear why Theadosia Berenson attended social functions alone or accompanied by this harridan of a chaperone. Peter resolved then and there that tonight he would keep Thea out at least five moments past midnight, even if he was so bored by that time the seconds dripped like molasses. ''I assure you, Mrs. Carey, my grandmother taught me to be a gentleman at all times, even under the most tempting of circumstances. Believe me, there's no need for you to worry. Thea will be perfectly safe with me.''

Davinia frowned at him, obviously unconvinced of his sincerity, but then her gaze went past him to the doorway. ''Theadosia,'' she said. ''Come in. How many times do I have to remind you it's not polite for a lady to hover in a doorway? Come in, come in.'' She extended a veiny hand. ''You look lovely, dear. Doesn't she, Peter?''

Lovely wasn't the word for it. Thea looked bedraggled and miserably self-conscious. Her dress fit badly, at best, and covered her from high neck to midcalf in a dreary beige. Her hair was its normal mousey-brown, and looped haphazardly into a frazzled topknot that already showed signs of slip-sliding toward her left ear. The double strand of pearls she wore was too long to be stylish and too big to be simply a nice touch. Matching pearl earrings, too large for her pointy little face, studded her earlobes and were all but lost behind the black-frame glasses that sat halfway down her nose, which obscured her thick-lashed and luminous eyes. Neither jewelry nor glasses did anything to enhance her overall appearance. But if lying to a lady wasn't in any Gentleman's Handbook, diplomacy certainly was.

Peter rose instantly to his feet and offered her a warmly approving smile. "Hello, Thea," he said. "I can't tell you how happy I am to see you. I've been looking forward to this evening for days."

She ducked her head and said, "Hello, Peter," in a voice so soft it practically evaporated on contact with the air.

"Stand up straight," Davinia commanded and Thea straightened like a marionette. "Remember who you are, tonight, Theadosia. Peter has assured me he will take very good care of you."

For a second, Peter caught a glimpse of life in the eyes behind the heavy-rimmed glasses, a flicker of amusement as out of place in Thea's brown eyes as the ray of sunlight tentatively creeping in through a crack in the draperies. "Okay," Thea said in her meek and whispery voice and he decided all he'd seen was a reflection in the lens of her glasses.

"Shall we go?" He was suddenly anxious to get her outside, away from the gloom and suffocating presence of her grandmother, away from the weight of expectations that seemed to press down about them from all directions. "I put the top up on the car so your hair won't get blown all out of…place." He paused, wishing he'd left the top down. She might like to have the wind blowing through her hair for a change, and it wasn't as if her hairstyle relied much on staying in place as it was. "But if you'd prefer, I can put it down again."

"Certainly not," Davinia said firmly. "I've never understood why anyone would have one of those convertibles in the first place. They're dangerous and I can assure you, Peter, that Thea does not wish to arrive anywhere, particularly at a formal affair, looking as if she's had her head in a wind tunnel."

Peter thought she might prefer that to looking as if she'd combed her hair with an egg beater, but since Thea didn't contradict her grandmother, he didn't think it was his place to step in and do it. Gentlemen, as a general rule, minded their own business.

He started to take Thea's elbow, but thought that if she didn't faint from nervousness at his touch, her grandmother might slap his hand with a ruler and remind him that a gentleman never touched a lady without permission. He hedged his bets by moving to the doorway and sort of urging Thea along by example. "Good evening, Mrs. Carey," he said.

"I do hope you have an enjoyable evening," the old woman called after them.

But Peter was almost positive she didn't mean a word of it.

Chapter Two

"Would you like something else to drink?" Peter asked as considerately as if it were the first time he'd posed a similar question instead of the eleventh or twelfth. "More punch, maybe? Or a soda?"

Thea tried to think of a witty reply, some way of refusing his offer that wouldn't be completely flat and uninteresting. Peter had been so nice, had tried so hard, right from the minute he'd opened the door of his car for her and offered for the second time to put down the convertible's top. She'd wanted to flash a saucy smile and say, *"Yes, please, I love the feel of the wind in my hair. I've always thought I'd enjoy driving a convertible. What about letting me test-drive this one? I promise I'll pay for the speeding ticket, if we get caught."*

But she hadn't said that. Not even close. She'd mumbled a simple, *"No, thank you,"* which had pretty much been the extent of her contribution to the conversation throughout the evening, with the occasional *"Yes, thank you,"* thrown in for variety.

"Would you like to sit here?"

"*Yes, thank you.*"

"*Shall I ask the waiter to get you another piece of wedding cake?*"

"*No, thank you.*"

"*Are you cold? Would you like to borrow my jacket?*"

"*No, thank you.*"

"*Do you want to dance?*"

"*No, thank you.*"

"No, thank you," she said now because as much as she wanted to say something else, *anything* else, she simply couldn't seem to get both brain and tongue working in sync. And, too, she couldn't bring herself to swallow another mouthful of punch. She was practically swimming in it already. The virgin punch, of course, the one made of sweet fruit juices and some fizzy water, served to the younger guests in lieu of champagne. Peter hadn't even asked her preference on that count, just indicated to their waiter that they'd both have the punch. Which meant either her grandmother had given him a stern warning about the dangers of drinking and dating, or he'd just assumed she didn't touch anything stronger than root beer and since she didn't, he wouldn't, either.

Or he might simply be afraid of what would happen if she got a little alcohol in her. She'd overheard her grandmother's embarrassing instruction to him to return her to Grace Place "in the same virtuous condition as when she'd walked out the door." With a soft sigh, Thea acknowledged there wasn't a chance in ten million the evening could end any other way. Alcohol or no.

"Dinner was good," she said, because the Peking duck had been cooked to perfection, and because she was determined to make at least one remark without being prompted.

He smiled, seemingly pleased she'd made even that small effort. "Yes, it was," he agreed. "I heard they brought in a hot new chef from the West Coast just for the occasion."

Thea thought *"bringing in a chef"* smacked of flaunting one's wealth, something no descendent of Davis Madison Grace would ever consider to be in good taste. "Imagine how far they had to go to find the duck," she said.

Peter blinked. And then he laughed, startling Thea with the pure sensual pleasure contained in that one throaty sound. She felt the heat of a blush rise in her cheeks, wondered if she'd actually said something amusing or if he was just being polite. Either possibility seemed equally disturbing and produced the exact same effect...freezing her ability to speak all over again.

"It wouldn't surprise me if they flew them in special delivery from Beijing," Peter said with a grin. "Her dad once told me he would spare no expense when it came to Angela's wedding."

Thea knew Peter and Angela had once been an item in the society columns, and it was no secret that the Merchants had hoped for a match between their family and the Braddocks. There had even been rumors late last year that Peter and Angela were unofficially engaged. Of course, there had been rumors before. About all of the Braddocks. But Thea had mainly only paid attention to the ones about Peter. He was closer to her age, twenty-seven to her twenty-five, and of the three brothers, she liked him the best.

Not that he would know this.

She took a deep breath and decided that as this was likely to be her only date ever with Peter Braddock, she ought to make a legitimate attempt to talk to him. No matter how difficult it was to open her mouth and say the words.

She did know how to talk and she never lacked for conversation when it was just her and her menagerie of pets. She'd been on dates before, too. Not many, true. Fewer, in fact, than she could count on both hands, but enough to know the rudiments of dialogue with a man. If she asked the right question, he'd start talking, then she'd mostly just have to nod and listen from there on in. She was good at listening. It was just getting the conversation started that caused her all the problems.

She wished she had said, yes, and let him walk to the bar and fetch her a soda. At least, then, she'd have had a few minutes to think about what she could say when he got back. But she didn't drink sodas. Bad for her teeth, her grandmother said. Bad for her skin. And no matter what she thought of to say when he returned with the soda, she'd be preoccupied in trying to hide the fact that she wasn't drinking the soda she'd requested he get for her.

Thea shifted in her chair and smoothed her beige silk skirt over her knees. She knew she looked lifeless and drab in the dress, knew it was hardly the height of contemporary fashion, knew even if she were wearing the gorgeous dress Miranda Danville had on at this very moment, she'd still look like the misfit she was. Peter must be wishing he could be anywhere else, with anyone else, doing anything other than sitting with her in this ungainly silence. He had to be counting the minutes until he could take her home.

But none of that bothered her as much as knowing that if she didn't say something soon, the evening would be over and he'd never know she actually had something to say.

"Wait just a minute," Peter said, interrupting her fierce struggle to conquer her inept silence. He leaned close and her senses were suddenly filled with him. His scent was a breezy blend of good soap and men's cologne; his roughly handsome face was near enough for her to see the sensual green of his eyes and the slight scar on the bridge of his otherwise perfect nose; his breath on her skin was warm against her cheek and as soft as a caress; his hand was firm and persuasive as he stood and urged her up out of her chair; his smile was as seductive as a kiss. "You have to dance with me now, Thea. Listen to that. They're playing our song."

She cocked her head to listen, sure he was teasing

her, wishing he would either go off and dance with someone else or be content to sit out the dances, wondering why he'd agreed to spend this intolerable evening with her in the first place. She'd noticed the covert glances of other wedding guests, knew most of them were looking at Peter with sympathy and admiring him for being too much of a gentleman to ditch his sad sack of a date and enjoy himself.

Thea wanted to tell him she'd honestly tried to override her grandmother's insistence that she accept his invitation. She wanted to say that just because his grandfather had coerced him into escorting her, didn't mean she expected him to entertain her. But then, slipping in between her melancholy thoughts, finding a foothold in her memory, the melody and lyrics of the song registered as familiar and coaxed a slow smile across her lips.

"You say it best," the lead singer crooned, *"when you say nothing at all."*

She glanced up at his face, hoping he wasn't making a joke at her expense. It had happened before. Not with Peter, but… Nothing in his expression suggested anything other than a kind attempt to let her know it was okay, that she didn't have to say anything at all. His smile—the one that was tucked in at the corners of his mouth and reflected in the true green of his eyes, was merely approving and, perhaps, just a little bit hopeful.

And without a second's warning, she was locked with Peter in a moment that meant something only to the two of them. He was teasing her and, for the first time in her life, Thea felt she was *in* on a joke. An amazing sense of belonging flooded through her, her throat lost its strangling tightness, and she laughed aloud. Softly, uncertainly…yes. Under her breath for the most part, but still a laugh that came right from the very heart of her.

Peter laughed, too, and looked…well, satisfied. "So, Theadosia," he said. "May I please have this dance?"

"Yes, thank you," she replied, feeling that somehow those three words were really all she needed to say.

IT WASN'T THE BEST TIME Peter had ever had at a wedding. That would have been Bryce's and Lara's wedding last month, with Adam's and Katie's wedding three months before that, running a close second. But tonight wasn't the worst time he'd ever had watching someone else get married, either. That would have been Christina Ephraim's wedding when he was fifteen and so hopelessly infatuated with the bride—his English tutor and drama coach *and* a sophisticated, beautiful older woman, besides—he'd very nearly embarrassed himself along with the whole Braddock family by sobbing out his heartache during the ceremony.

Luckily, his grandmother had sensed his distress and developed a dizzy spell that required him to step outside with her until her equilibrium—and his composure—returned. He'd always loved Grandmother Jane for that, and because she'd never said a word about it afterward, even though he knew she didn't have dizzy spells. Ever.

Yes, that was definitely the worst wedding he'd ever attended. Tonight, with Thea? Not even close. In fact, if he could just get her to relax a little, they might both actually start to enjoy the evening.

Well, okay, so true enjoyment might be a stretch, but at least *he'd* have a better time if she wasn't so quietly miserable. He'd never spent this much concentrated effort on a date before and would have been angry about her lack of response if it hadn't been Thea. It wasn't that he felt sorry for her—something about her didn't allow for pity. It was more that he wanted to put her at ease, wanted her to have a good time, wanted this night to be a pleasant evening for her to remember.

Before at other social functions, he'd danced with her because common courtesy demanded it. He'd tried to be charming because he thought her life was a tad lacking in the charm department. But now that he'd been inside Grace Place and felt Davinia Carey's suffocating disapproval firsthand, he wanted to go beyond courtesy and easy charm to show Thea a good time. That seemed important now that he knew he would soon have to take her back to a dark, dreary place where she was told to stand up straight and reminded at every turn to act like a lady. A place where smiles and laughter were probably scarce, and bestowed even less often than any genuine approval.

So if she didn't find talking to him an easy thing to

do, he had to consider that a personal challenge, not as some great flaw in her. And as long as they were dancing, the lack of conversation didn't feel so cumbersome. It was obvious she was nervous. And shy. And trying to juggle who knew how many edicts from her grandmother about how she should behave. It wouldn't surprise him in the least if Davinia had spies posted around the country club even now, watching Thea, waiting to report any untoward act or unladylike behavior. No one deserved to be treated that way and he really would have liked to ask Thea why she put up with the old tyrant.

But that would only put her in an even more awkward position and probably put the kiss of death on any further conversation for the night.

As if that would be so different from now.

The best he could do was allow her her silence. So he merely pulled her a little closer and marveled at how well she danced. She always seemed so uncomfortable in social settings, so ill at ease with herself and others, but on the dance floor, she moved almost...well, gracefully. Sometimes, like now, when she forgot for a minute to be self-conscious, she floated in his arms like a feather. "We dance very well together, Thea," he said, surprised to realize it was true.

She missed a step and looked up at him, clearly startled and blushing at the compliment, which brought a pleasing hint of color to the smooth ivory skin beneath the oversized glasses. "Oh," she said. "Then I must be doing it wrong."

"No, you must be doing it right."

She shook her head, still looking up at him, and he noticed, maybe for the first time, that her eyes were a warm, rich coffee-brown, fringed with a smudge of dark lashes. "If I'm doing it correctly, no one's *supposed* to notice." She bit her lip, as if so many words in one sentence were a faux pas. "According to Miss Blythe."

Peter drew back slightly to look at her. "You took dancing from Miss Blythe, too?"

She made a face and ducked her head as she nodded. Her voice, when it came, was quieter even than before, shyer and softer. "I was in your class once."

He wanted to remember, to call up some long forgotten memory of Thea at what age? Seven? Eight? He hadn't been more than ten or eleven when his grandmother had enrolled him at Miss Blythe's. Just for the fundamentals, Grandmother Jane had said and, true to her word, she hadn't pushed him beyond the essentials of learning the basic steps. He could conjure up a mental picture of Miranda Danville, her blond braids dangling across her shoulders, as she told him to *count his steps!* He could recall Angela Merchant, her blond curls bouncing down her back, insisting he'd stepped on her toes *on purpose!* He could remember a whole chorus of pretty little girls, who knew, even then, who they were and who weren't at all sure this rough and tumble boy belonged in their social strata—even if his newly acquired name was Braddock. They'd changed their minds and found him immensely acceptable by the time adolescence rounded their bodies and added an alluring charm to their flirtation skills.

But he didn't remember Thea.

"I didn't take classes with Miss Blythe for very long," he said, as if that excused it. "I wasn't exactly star pupil material at that time in my life."

"You were a natural, even then," Thea stated. "Even Miss Blythe thought so."

He laughed. "I'm afraid not. She told me flat out to concentrate on developing some charm because I certainly wasn't going to get anywhere with my dancing."

"Did your grandmother know she said that?"

Jane Braddock would have taken the shine right off of Miss Blythe's fancy dancing shoes if she'd known. "No," he said with a self-effacing smile. "I didn't want to take dance lessons in the first place. If Miss Blythe hadn't said that to me, I might never have decided to prove her wrong. Then where would I be right now?" He pulled her closer. "I'd be sitting on the sidelines, watching you dance with some other man and wishing it were me."

She stumbled and he caught her, setting her back into the shared rhythm of the dance as easily as if she hadn't missed a step. "Don't please," she said so softly he had to bend his head to catch the words. "You don't have to charm me. Couldn't we just... dance?"

A stab of remorse whispered through him like a shameful secret. Thea knew his words were false, recognized his charm for the polished insincerity it was, and was offended by it. As she had every right to be. This *date* hadn't been his idea, true. But he didn't for a minute believe it had been high on her wish list, either. She didn't want him to pretend. She simply wanted the evening to proceed to its natural end with some little bit of dignity.

"That would be my pleasure," he said because, whether she believed him or not, that much was true.

"YOU WON'T REGRET THIS, Mrs. Fairchild." Ainsley Danville hugged Ilsa with one hundred percent pure enthusiasm. "I'm very good with people and I have a real knack for matchmaking. Even if I do say so myself." She drew back, her pretty face flushed with excitement, her blue eyes sparkling with anticipation. "Who do you think should be my first client?"

Ilsa tried not to sigh. "You'll start in the office and learn about all the paperwork that goes along with this kind of work. And Ainsley, you must keep in mind that discretion is essential. I'd prefer you tell anyone who asks that you're an associate with IF Enterprises, *not* a matchmaker. For the record, I seldom, if ever, refer to my business as 'matchmaking.'"

"I understand completely, Mrs. Fairchild. I am the very *soul* of discretion." Her smile bloomed again and Ilsa thought it more than likely the news that she'd hired an assistant would be all over Rhode Island before sundown tomorrow. Perhaps all over New England, as well. But it was done. She'd wrestled with this decision for weeks. Ainsley had been campaigning for the job for nearly a year. Ilsa could only hope having an apprentice would turn out to be a lucky decision, even if it didn't feel at all like a wise one at the moment.

Ainsley leaned closer. "Tell me, please, Mrs. Fairchild, are you responsible for today's wedding, too?"

They were both in attendance at the wedding reception for Angela Merchant and Park Overton—now Mr. and Mrs. Park Overton—and Ilsa actually had made an *introduction of possibilities* for the couple not quite a year ago. But responsible for the wedding? No, she wouldn't say that at all. "I don't take credit for weddings, Ainsley. Only for helping someone see possibilities that already existed in the first place. I do hope you'll keep in mind that no matter how well you do your homework or how sure you are the match you've put together is the right one, the whole thing can, and often does, fall apart. Park and Angela are two of the lucky ones. Much of what happens is luck, Ainsley. Once we've introduced the possibility of a match, the rest is out of our sphere of influence entirely. So while I don't believe in taking credit for someone else's happily ever after, I certainly don't believe in blaming myself when a match doesn't work out, either."

Ainsley nodded, her expression beautifully serious. "I'll remember that," she said. "No taking the credit and no taking the blame." Her irrepressible spirit rebounded with a wide smile. "So how soon can I start? Because I already have someone in mind as sort of a test case. My cousin, Scott, is single and desperately lonely. I have a hunch Julia Butterfield would really like him. He's sort of rowdy and he's not a vegan—he eats all kinds of meat—but I think he might change his bad habits if he met the right woman.''

Ilsa kept smiling despite the most pressing impulse to sigh. "First, office procedure, Ainsley," she reminded her new assistant. "Then we'll see about letting you work with me on a match."

"Okay. Gotcha."

Ilsa reminded herself again that she needed help with her business. And Ainsley had the personality for it. She was cute, she was bubbly, she was optimistic and she had a natural intuition about people, even though it flared a little on the wild side occasionally. But Ilsa did hope this new alliance would work out. She needed an infusion of Ainsley's enthusiasm. Her own had been flagging lately and this could turn out well for both of them. After all, the whole premise of IF Enterprises was summed up in her own personal motto that Anything Is Possible.

Sipping her glass of wine, Ilsa looked around to see what Peter had done with Thea. They were no longer sitting in the far corner of the room, the spot Thea seemed usually to prefer and which they had occupied since dinner. They might already have left. It was early yet, but...no, there. They were dancing, and despite the fact that Theadosia looked like a maiden aunt, she seemed to be...well, not entirely miserable. Peter didn't appear to be bored to distraction, although it was hard to tell for sure, and common sense told her he couldn't be enjoying the evening.

Maybe something would come of this, although she couldn't imagine what. Or how. Ilsa simply felt badly about her part in putting this mismatch together. Even for just these few hours. She should never have mentioned the impulse to Archer. She should not have heeded his encouragement to follow through on her hunch and set up this one *evening of possibility*. And she definitely should not have allowed him to use his influence over Peter and his long acquaintance with Davinia Carey to arrange this date with disaster. What possibility could exist, other than in her imagination, between Peter Braddock and Theadosia Berenson? It was a bad idea that just wouldn't go away.

"Ainsley?" she said on impulse. "What do you know about Thea Berenson?"

Ainsley frowned, studying the question the way she might examine a raw turnip. "Well, some people call her Teddy Bear because she always looks a little fuzzy, if you know what I mean?"

Ilsa did.

"I've heard her called a poor, little rich girl, too, but it would be hard to tell that by looking at her. I don't know what happened to her parents, although it must have been bad because nobody ever mentions them except in hushed-up tones, like it was some big scandal or something. She had a brother, but he died a couple of years ago. Of meanness, my sister said, but I think it was really just a heart attack. No mystery there. The real mystery to me,'' Ainsley added as if it were incomprehensible, ''is why she still lives with her grandmother who is—pardon my frankness, but I have to be honest—the original Wicked Witch of all New England and possibly the world.''

There was some truth in the statement, but while Ilsa didn't want to discourage her protégé's observations, she did want to encourage a temperate perspective of others' life situations. ''Davinia Carey isn't, perhaps, a warm person, but I believe she has had a rather unhappy life.''

''Well, excuse me,'' Ainsley said without apology. ''But that's not a good reason to make Thea miserable.''

Also true.

''Why do you think Thea allows someone else to make her miserable?'' Ilsa asked, interested in gaining someone else's insight. ''If, indeed, she is.''

''Oh, how could she not be?'' Ainsley said. ''I can't imagine why she stays at Grace Place when she can afford to buy a place of her own.''

''Maybe her money is tied up in trusts and she can't touch any of it until she's older.'' Ilsa had a file on Thea—a woefully thin one—but of course, the financial information was private, so all she could do was speculate along with Ainsley. ''That's very possible.''

''She could get a job. She has a degree from Wellesley, you know. I don't know what she studied, but she could get a job at a museum or something. I sure wouldn't live in that dark old house with that old...''

Ainsley let the intended epithet trail away. "With her grandmother," she finished and Ilsa gave her full marks for being a quick learner.

"Maybe," Ilsa said, "Thea is afraid of what will happen if she leaves."

"Maybe with good reason." Ainsley frowned, obviously still studying the oddness of Thea's life. But then, like the sun coming out, her blue eyes went wide and she turned back to Ilsa, the light of conspiracy in her smile. "Holy Toledo, Mrs. Carey didn't hire you to make a match for Thea, did she? I mean, who would you ever find to match up with her?"

A good question, if not quite an accurate observation. "There's someone for everyone, Ainsley."

"He'll have to be a true Prince Charming," she said, her attention returning to the couples on the dance floor, as if she thought she could spot a match for Thea just by looking. "And maybe very nearsighted."

Ilsa let her gaze travel back to where Peter and Thea were still dancing. Not talking. Or looking at each other. But something in the way he held her, something in the way she moved in his arms, something about...

No. Ilsa knew she had to be imagining that indefinable *something* she felt when she saw Peter with Thea. They could never, in a million years, find the true heart of the other. Even if they were inclined to look.

"Ilsa?" Ainsley's voice had softened to a thoughtful musing. "Have you ever felt that maybe Thea and..."

She didn't finish the thought, left it dangling in the air between them, but the quicksilver clench of knowing caught Ilsa unaware. *Peter*. Ainsley felt it, too. That *something* Ilsa hadn't been able to name.

Which didn't mean either one of them were right about it.

"Davinia has not hired me to find a match for Thea," Ilsa said truthfully. "Nor would she. Ever."

Ainsley smiled, secretively at first, but then with blinding self-confidence. "Would you mind if I worked on a possibility for Thea?" she asked. "On my own time, of course, and I won't actually *do* anything. I'll just sort of think about it, look around for a nearsighted prince of a guy, ponder possibilities in my head. Would that be okay?"

Ilsa knew she should say no. Flat out. But Ainsley couldn't, just by thinking and wondering and imagining, do any harm. Truthfully, she couldn't do any worse than Ilsa had already done if she set out full-tilt to find Thea a match. "As long as you keep in mind that even a matchmaker can't work miracles."

"Gotcha," Ainsley said, although a miracle was clearly what she had in mind.

Chapter Three

Peter didn't ask again if she wanted him to put down the top of the convertible. He just did it.

He didn't ask if she wanted to head down to Point Judith, either. He simply turned the Beemer in that direction and drove.

He didn't offer much in the way of conversation, just asked if the wind was too much, if she felt chilly, if she didn't think this was one of those nights when the earth and the sky were in perfect accord.

To which she answered, respectively, with two separate shakes of her head and a singular nod. She didn't say that the wind felt glorious on her face and in its wild fling with her hair. She didn't say that she loved the faint nip of autumn in the air and the brewing fragrance of a distant storm. She didn't confess that she, too, thought this was one of those perfect nights, which, in some mysterious alignment of nature, occasionally happened in a New England autumn. And she especially didn't say that ensconced in the deep leather seat, her head resting against the headrest, her feet flat on the floor, sitting as close as she ever sat to another person and riding through the dark with the night rushing over her in an endless sensual wave, felt daring and somehow, extraordinarily brave.

Thea didn't want to spoil the moment with words for fear Peter would remember who he was with, turn the car around and take her straight home. So she just closed her eyes and let the sensations weave their way through her with all their myriad pleasures.

When he stopped the car and shut off the engine, she heard the Atlantic chanting its rhythmic poetry to the rocky shores around Point Judith. She kept her eyes shut, recognized their location from the road they'd traveled and from the pulsating blink of the lighthouse which crept beneath her lashes and lightened the darkness every few seconds. The scent of the ocean surrounded them, more ancient than the forest primeval, its song as familiar and as soothing as a heartbeat.

"Thea?" Peter's voice was soft as the night, almost as if he thought she really might be asleep.

"Peter," she replied to let him know she was awake and aware, even if her eyes were still closed. There, in a darkness of her own making, she could drink in the fantasy of being alone with him, imagining for the space of a single breath that he wanted to be here with her, that he planned to kiss her senseless in full view of a million stars, that he had brought her here on this special night to make love to her with the eternal ocean as witness.

"We're at Point Judith Lighthouse," he said.

"I know. Did you get lost?"

"No."

"Point Judith isn't exactly on the way to Grace Place."

"No, it isn't."

She nodded and the thought flitted through her mind that she might have read Peter wrong, that it was possible he hid a lecherous soul beneath his handsome face and gentlemanly manners. No matter how she dressed, or acted, or how hard she tried to make herself invisible, there were still men who thought they could take advantage. But Peter could have any woman he wanted. He was Hollywood handsome, deathly charming and rich as Croesus. He could have no design on her fortune or her figure. He probably didn't even realize she *had* a figure beneath the shapeless clothes she wore.

But she trusted Peter, for no particular reason other than he had always been nicer to her than he had to be. He was being polite, stopping here, pretending in his gentlemanly way that he was in no rush to take her home. The idea he could want anything more was without substance and evaporated like so much wistful thinking into the cool night air.

"I'll take you home, if you prefer."

She opened her eyes then, to see the moonlight as it flared across the water and played tag with the surf. They were parked in an open area just off the narrow road, the only car in sight, so the night and the ocean were theirs for the moment. Thea rather liked the idea of that. She liked being with Peter and feeling, if not completely relaxed in his company, at least, at ease with him. She'd been to this particular place on Point Judith before—always in daylight and always alone— but here, on this same road. The rocks below were a good place to sketch, a good place to daydream. It felt right, somehow, to be here with him now, although her grandmother would have a fit if she knew.

"Bryce taught me to surf right out there," Peter said into the quiet. "The first real wave I caught took me straight into the rocks and smashed up my board pretty good. I had scrapes and bruises from top to bottom, but I was hooked." A moment ticked past and then another. "Have you ever been surfing, Thea?"

She smiled, a soft rush of humor curving through her at the thought of being in the water, straddling a surfboard, waiting for the perfect wave. "I don't even own a swimsuit," she said.

He turned in the seat, brushing her hand with his thigh in the process, and sending pinpoints of heat scattering like naughty desires across her nerve endings. She pulled her hand back too quickly, making something out of nothing and feeling foolish in the process.

"Please tell me you're kidding," he said, sounding equally earnest and appalled at the possibility.

She shook her head, embarrassed. "A lady doesn't kid."

"Ladies do, however, swim."

"Well, I don't."

He considered that in silence while she wished she'd

never opened her mouth. She didn't want to talk about herself. He surely didn't want to talk about her, either. Why hadn't she asked him about surfing, or architecture, or what he thought about the space program, or any topic at all other than swimsuits?

"May I ask why?"

Now it was personal and a subject her grandmother had said was restricted to family. A lady didn't discuss the tragedies of her life, nor did she open herself to questions about her past. Those things were private. But Thea was torn between her grandmother's doctrines and her own—suddenly very strong—desire to explain to Peter why she was so different, why she had never once in her life put on a swimsuit. "My mother drowned."

The words hung there. Then with an urgency she couldn't suppress, more words came out, as if she'd breached the dam and could no longer hold them in. "Grandmother said it was her own fault. I was only a baby and don't really know what happened, except that Mother was wild and reckless and she drank. A lot. She did other things, too. Grandmother won't talk about them. She just says my mother went out on the yacht with some people she shouldn't have and did very unladylike things, and that sometime during the party, she fell overboard and drowned. Nobody on the deck could remember how it happened or even exactly when." Thea bit her lip, horrified at what she'd told, and amazed at how good it felt to have finally said the forbidden thing aloud. "It was a long time ago," she added, as if that explained away her relief. "Grandmother doesn't like for me to talk about it, but that's why I don't swim."

She could feel his eyes on her in the dark and she was ashamed for blabbering like an idiot about something he couldn't possibly be interested in knowing.

"I'm sorry, Thea," he said. "It's tough to lose your mother, no matter how old you are when it happens."

His sympathetic tone washed over her, but the only response she seemed able to make was a half-hearted shrug, as if it didn't matter.

"I know when my mother died, no one wanted to talk to me about it, either. At the time, I thought it wasn't polite or something, but now I realize that the adults in my life simply didn't know what to say, so basically they didn't say anything at all." He paused. "My grandmother was the only one who encouraged me to talk and to remember my mother as she was."

"My grandmother was ashamed," Thea said, hardly realizing it as the truth until the words were out. "She still is."

There wasn't anything he could say to refute the claim and Thea was glad he didn't try. He was leaning against the driver's side door with his right hand extended along the back of the seat and, with just a slight stretch, his fingers brushed a tumbled strand of her hair. It was a gesture of understanding and simple kindness, catching her unprepared and vulnerable; leaving her breathless and bereft in its wake. "Your hair got all windblown," he said softly.

Self-consciously, she lifted a hand to fuss with the mousy tendrils, defeated by the fine, limp strands and a serious lack of style before she even made the effort. "I must look awful," she said, aware as she had never been before of her unkempt and ugly appearance.

"Moonlight becomes you, Thea."

He was a gallant liar, a thief of hearts. She knew that, yet the thrill went deep inside her and spread its warmth like melting butter. "It's getting late," she said. "You probably ought to take me home."

"It's still early, barely eleven." His smile teased her in the dusky moonlight. "And you have yet to make a wish on one of those stars."

She looked up into the canopy of distant suns, with all their accompanying celestial bodies, and wished someday, somehow, in a perfect universe, that a man like Peter Braddock might fall in love with her. "If I did make a wish, I couldn't tell you."

"Why not?"

"Because wishes are private and personal and a gentleman really shouldn't ask a lady to tell her secrets."

"You know, Thea, between all the things a lady isn't supposed to do and all the things a gentleman isn't supposed to ask, it's a wonder the human race is still in existence."

Smiling, she let her head drop back against the headrest, the better to see the stars. "It's always been a mystery to me why anyone would want to be a lady. Or a gentleman for that matter."

He laughed gently in the dark. "I'm not sure there are that many of us left in the world."

She liked that he considered himself a gentleman. Too few men did these days. But right now, she wished with all her heart he'd make a pass at her. Just one. Just so she'd know what it was like for one instant to be the object of his desire. A sigh slipped past her lips, dreary with reality. "Why did you bring me here, Peter?"

He gave her query a moment's consideration. "Because this night is too gorgeous to waste on sleep. Because the ocean was here waiting for us. Because it's too early to take you home. Because I'd like to hear you laugh before the evening ends."

"I didn't think I'd asked a multiple choice question."

"It isn't complicated, Thea. I wanted you to see Point Judith by moonlight, that's all."

She thought it was probably simpler even than that. Peter knew—as everyone knew—that she wouldn't, in her whole life, get many opportunities to ride shotgun in a convertible on a moonstruck night. He wanted her to have the experience, to feel the wind in her hair, the rush of air on her face, the sweet seduction of speeding like light through the darkness. That was certainly simple enough. And kind. In its way. She wished…oh, a thousand wishes as unobtainable as the stars, but mostly that she hadn't asked him why. It was better to live in the moment and not cloud the evening with questions that could only have answers she didn't want to hear.

"I come here sometimes to sketch," she said. "Usually early in the morning when I don't have to jockey with the surfers for a parking space or an unobstructed view."

"It's a popular spot," Peter agreed. "What do you sketch?"

She imagined drawing them—the convertible, the lighthouse, the ocean, the moonlight… Peter, with his dark hair tousled, his handsome brow, his easy smile. Maybe she'd put herself in the convertible with him. But probably not. It would be nicer to just imagine herself as she wished she were, instead of looking at a sketch and seeing at a glance all the many ways she didn't fit into the picture. "I draw whatever I see. Rocks, the lighthouse, seagulls, sandpipers, people, if there are any around. It's more pleasure than art."

"I never thought of you as an artist," he said, then seemed to realize how that sounded. "I mean, I never thought of you as *not* an artist, either. It's just that…"

He never actually *thought* about her at all. Thea knew that's what he was trying not to say. "I'm not an artist," she said. "I sketch because I enjoy doing it. I imagine it's much the same as you feel about surfing."

"Used to feel," he corrected, his gaze turning once again to the frothy waves. "There doesn't seem to be much time for it anymore. And I suppose, to be honest,

I've outgrown the thrill...even though once upon a time, riding a wave was as sweet as a lover's kiss."

The thrill transferred from his memory to her imagination and formed a longing that moved through her like the incoming tide. *As sweet as a lover's kiss....* Not that she would ever know either thrill. But, somehow, just hearing him say the words opened a cavern of regret in her soul and she wished he'd never brought her here, never been nice to her, never let her catch an instant's glimpse of what she could never hope to know.

Far out at sea, the lights of a ship blinked once, twice, then vanished into the darkness. Overhead, a bank of clouds slipped over the silver moon, obscuring it with a lethal silence, in much the same way her disappointment and anger passed over her then turned itself—without a single intelligent reason—on Peter. "I'd like to go home now," she said tightly.

He didn't answer and she thought, perhaps, he might refuse to take her, might try to persuade her to change her mind, might ask her what was wrong. But he merely exhaled softly. Probably a sigh of relief that this awful *date* was nearly over.

"I guess that means you're not going to tell me your wish."

"I *wished* to go home."

She felt his eyes on her, questioning, uncertain, and she felt the tug of an attraction that was as one-sided as it was ridiculous, and as strong as the self-inflicted anger stirring up a tempest inside her heart. She had no business here on this rocky beach with Peter Braddock. He had no business being here with her, either. He belonged with someone blond and beautiful, someone confident and compelling—someone Thea would never be.

And she belonged at Grace Place where she was loved to distraction by her cats.

"All right, we'll go," he said, shifting in the seat and reaching down to switch on the ignition. "I'd better put the top up before we start back, though. Sounds like we could run into some rain on the drive home."

The storm that had been just a huddle of grumbling clouds on the horizon, now stirred the air and agitated the waves, bringing with it a far off roll of thunder and the rising scent of a coming rain.

Thea wished he'd leave the top down, despite the possibility of getting drenched. It would, she thought, be a fitting end to this odd evening to arrive home as soggy as she was miserable.

But of course, she didn't say that, either.

PETER TALKED ALL THE way back.

He talked about Bryce and Lara. He talked about Adam and Katie. He talked about deeds and misdeeds committed by the Braddock brothers growing up. He talked about the mischief he liked to plot with his soon-to-be-official nephew, Cal. He doubled up on the charm, concentrated a considerable effort on engaging Thea in some form of conversation, and got exactly nowhere for his trouble... Unless he counted the few monosyllables she uttered when he asked a point-blank question.

"Are you warm enough?"

"Yes."

"Would you like to stop for a drink?"

"No."

"How about ice cream?"

"No."

"Everything okay?"

"Fine."

She huddled against the passenger-side door, like a scolded child who believes if she can just be quiet enough and still enough no one will notice she's there at all.

With anyone else, Peter would have let frustration take its natural course and fallen into an indifferent silence. But he couldn't imagine this happening with anyone else. The women he dated wanted to be with him. They held up their end of the conversation. They asked questions, they were avidly interested in hearing his answers. They smiled, they laughed, they made an effort to engage his attention and pique his interest. But Thea was only his date by default and, although he wished it could be otherwise, Peter knew she was as aware of that fact as he.

He felt the complexity of her mood—its anger and apology, its aggrieved humility—and couldn't begin to imagine what, if anything, he could have done to cause it. Or maybe it had nothing at all to do with him. Maybe she dreaded going home, despite her insistence on going there. Or maybe sudden storms made her moody and anxious. The rain had started with a few fat splatters soon after he'd put the top up and driven away from Point Judith and now the windshield wipers were working at top speed to clear away the steady downpour.

For the twenty minutes it took to reach the turnoff and pass between the scrolled iron gates of Grace Place, Peter said whatever he could think of to ease her obvious unease, with no visible results. He couldn't help but think she was cold, huddled as she was against the door. Reaching down, he flicked the heater to high, but that had little affect on the chilly atmosphere inside the car.

"Are you sure you're warm enough?" he asked.

"Yes," she said, her voice tight with misery.

Peter wished he could just feel sorry for Thea and be done with her. But pity required some sense of entitlement from the recipient and there simply was none. Maybe it was something about the set of her chin and the way she'd folded her arm across her lap, a gesture clearly meant to state *"Keep your sympathy. I neither want nor need it."* Or perhaps it had something to do with him knowing that she, too, had lost her mother in a tragic manner. The experience of being orphaned so suddenly and so unnecessarily gave them a common bond, an understanding of what it meant to be a motherless child.

Of course, his mother hadn't drowned and he'd never thought of her death as an accident. Peter believed his stepfather had always meant her harm in one form or another. That the death had come about accidentally didn't, in his mind, absolve the man from guilt. Still he'd had James to rescue him, grandparents to welcome him home, brothers to emulate and admire.

How different would Thea's life have been, how different might *she* be now, if she'd been taken in by a loving family, instead of a critical and cold Davinia Grace Carey? Surely then, she wouldn't have the look of someone who carried the weight of heavy responsibility on her thin shoulders.

Grace Place came into view, a gloomy fortress with too many dark windows and too few lights left burning to welcome a traveler home.

Peter slowed the car, hating worse than anything to deliver Thea to such a place.

"Thank you, Peter," she said in a rush even before the BMW roadster came to a complete stop, the words tumbling over themselves to be heard, coming out insincere and angrily polite. "It was a lovely evening and I appreciate your kindness."

Shifting quickly into Neutral, he shut off the engine and watched in complete bewilderment as she fumbled with the door handle. "It locks automatically," he explained, reaching for the control switch. But his finger paused on the lever. He was at a loss to understand her hurry and couldn't begin to imagine what was going through her mind. She couldn't be afraid he'd try to kiss her good-night, could she? "If you'll wait a minute, Thea, I'll walk you to the door so you won't get wet.''

Her shoulders sagged as if his words had somehow defeated her urgency. "You would, of course, have an umbrella."

"There's always one in the car."

Her sigh was brief and poignant. "Look, Peter, there's no reason for you to get wet. Thank you for the evening and now, if you'll unlock my door, I'll leave you in peace."

Now what in hell had brought this on? "If I've inadvertently said something to upset you, Thea, please accept my apology, but I am going to see you safely inside, even if we both get drenched."

The Beemer's interior light stayed on automatically for several seconds after the engine was turned off and in the soft light, with the rain slickly coating the windows, confining them in the intimate space, she looked small and appealing and almost attractive. "That isn't necessary," she said.

There was a note of pleading in her voice and he offered a smile to reassure her, in case reassurance was what she needed. "Seeing a young lady to her door is a gentleman's duty and privilege."

The overhead light blinked out, but Peter would have sworn he saw a flash of resentment in her eyes, although it had to have been merely an instant's reflection in the lens of her dark-rimmed glasses. "Then by all means," she said tautly. "Get your umbrella and see me to the door."

He hesitated, wondering again what he'd said. "I'd like to know what I've done to upset you."

"Nothing, Peter. You've done nothing." Her hands twisted a wrinkle into the skirt of her shapeless dress. "You've been a perfect gentleman all evening, but it's getting very late and I'd like to go inside if you'll just let me out of your car."

He pressed the release, heard the soft *pop* as the locks clicked open, and half expected her to make a dash for the house before he could grab the umbrella and get out of the car.

But she waited for him, letting him come around to the passenger's side and open the door for her. She stepped out, ducked under the umbrella's cover and together they ran for the front steps of Grace Place to the shelter of the darkened portico.

Once safely there, Peter shook the umbrella and snapped it closed, but when he turned to say good-night to Thea, she was already disappearing into the cavernous gloom. Without saying good-night or goodbye, she slipped inside, the heavy wooden panel closed behind her and Peter found himself with the door shut quietly, but firmly, in his face.

He had a moment's impulse to laugh at the simple indignity, but he was too confused by her odd behavior to find anything funny about it. Nothing like this had ever happened to him before. He'd been dating since he was barely a teen and no other date had ever ended so abruptly or left him in such a rotten state of mind. What in Sam Hill had he done to her?

He'd returned her home before her grandmother's midnight curfew, despite his intention to keep her out late. Her virtue hadn't at any time tonight been compromised...or even tested. He'd done his best to be attentive. He'd actually even enjoyed the evening more than he'd have thought possible. True, he hadn't expected much, but then he'd never found Thea boring. He'd always thought of her reticence as a challenge and her lack of conversation as a choice, not an indication that she had nothing to say.

Turning, Peter looked out at the sodden night, trying to recall the evening and when, exactly, it had gone wrong and what, if anything, he might have done to prevent it. She'd seemed to have an okay time at the wedding. Well, at the reception, anyway, but who—other than the bride and groom and maybe their families—had a really great time during the actual wedding itself, anyway? Maybe Thea hadn't enjoyed the dinner. Maybe the duck had been too rich for her and upset her stomach. Maybe she'd had too much champagne punch or not enough. Maybe she was tired from all the dancing or from his persistent efforts to get her to talk. Maybe she didn't like the wind blowing her hair. Maybe she didn't like looking at the ocean at night. Maybe she didn't like sudden storms.

Or maybe, she just didn't like him.

Waiting for a lull in the storm, Peter leaned against one of the twin columns and watched as the rain came faster and harder than before. He considered the possibility that Thea resented this arranged date, that she resented him for seeing it through to its sad and soggy conclusion. He didn't blame her if that was the way she felt, but would she have been happier if he'd refused his grandfather's request? Would it have made a difference if her grandmother hadn't insisted she accept? Or perhaps Thea had wanted to go out with him and was disappointed with the reality of the evening.

How was he supposed to know if any of the possibilities occurring to him held any basis in fact? And what would he do about it, even if he did happen to alight on the truth? He couldn't save Thea, although after tonight, he had to admit someone certainly ought to do so. There was a certain noble appeal, too, in the idea of being a white knight to her damsel in distress.

On the other hand, Thea was no Sleeping Beauty, locked away in an ivory tower by her wicked old grandmother. She had money. She had a name nearly as old and honored as his own. She had an education, she'd graduated from Wellesley, or so he'd heard. She had intelligence—he knew *that* for a fact—even if she did seem to work pretty hard at keeping it under wraps. No, Thea didn't need some well-meaning, but misguided, man to save her. She was fully capable of saving herself. Why she didn't was another mystery altogether, but it was ridiculous for him to spend any more of his time worrying about her.

The rain let up by degrees, lessening its steady descent, and when it had slacked to a fine drizzle, Peter unfurled the umbrella again, calculating, as best he could in the dusky light—Davinia Carey certainly didn't waste any money on outside lighting—a feasible route around the puddles to the car.

"Kitty? Kitty, kitty, kitty?"

The voice floated like a birdcall somewhere near the treetops, soft as a whisper, soothing and familiar.

"Ally? Kitty, kitty?"

Peter went down the steps, looking up to the dark windows above. Whatever lights were on inside were curtained off from within so the front of the house remained brooding and dark. Forgetting the puddles, he moved across the lawn, still looking up, following the urgent whispers to the driveway, around to a long view of the east side of Grace Place.

"Darn it, Ally. How did you get out this time? Don't you know it's raining?"

Peter thought he heard a tiny, discontented mewling in reply and, as he came around the corner, he searched the shadows of the trees for the cat. It was too dark to make out such a small shape on such a large, dark branch, but there was no mistaking the very feminine shape in the lighted window. Well, in truth, he was going on speculation because until this minute he'd never known Thea Berenson actually *had* a shape, much less a very *nice* shape. At some time, on some level, of course, he must have noticed because he had danced with her and even if their bodies had never flirted with a close embrace, he had held her in his arms during many a song.

But he'd never seen her so clearly.

Or more probably, he'd never really looked. The

light pooling in the room behind her cast a perfect, rather enchanting, and impossible to miss, silhouette as she leaned out through the open window, her arms bracing her weight against the sill.

"Oh, Ally," she said. "Just look at you. You're soaked to the skin. Why on earth would you go out on a night like this?"

The cat mewed pitifully in response somewhere out among the tree limbs and Peter watched, fascinated as much by the sweet, soothing sound of Thea's voice as by the sight of her crawling through the window out onto an upper branch. She was minus shoes, a dress and any appearance of an inhibition. The best he could tell, she had on a slip that started just above her breasts and ended a long way shy of her knees. Its silky whiteness all but glowed in the dark and it was amazingly easy to follow her progress as she made her way along the branch. She crooned to the cat, reassuring it in rhythmic tones, and under the cover of her speech, Peter moved closer until he was below—several feet below—the sloping limb along which she crept.

Unnoticed as yet, he stood, a smile curving across his lips. Thea in a tree, risking life and limb to rescue a silly cat. Who would have thought she could be so foolishly brave? He wondered briefly if he should call out to her, but he didn't want to startle her. It occurred to him to climb the tree and offer to help in the rescue effort, but he'd need a ladder even to reach the lowest branch, which would require assistance from inside the house and he was quite sure Davinia Carey did not know—nor was there any need for her to know—that her granddaughter was up in a tree at midnight. And wearing only some rather form-fitting underwear.

Definitely better if Peter stayed quiet and close by...in case Thea needed help.

"Come on, Ally," she whispered hoarsely. "Make some effort, will you? It's wet and cold out here and rescuing you isn't nearly as much fun as it was the first five or six times you got yourself stuck in this tree." She inched along, her slip creeping slowly, but surely, up her thigh.

Peter couldn't have looked away if he'd tried.

The rain picked up its rhythm again, rustling first in the leaves of the oak before plopping with increasing insistence all around the outermost base of the tree. Still sheltered beneath the spreading branches, Peter moved with Thea, keeping her in sight as she got closer to where Ally, the cat, apparently waited to be rescued.

"See?" Thea said to the cat. "It's still raining and any minute now, we're both going to be soaked through to the skin. So please, crawl down here to me and let's get back inside. Come on, Ally. You can do it. Just a little bit farther...that's a good kitty."

There was a *crack,* a splintering jolt of a sound, as Peter stepped on a fallen, brittle limb and felt it snap into pieces beneath his shoe. He looked down, then up again as the silence from above warned him he'd blown his cover. "It's me, Thea," he said softly, not wishing to alarm her. "Peter."

"Peter?" Her voice lost its confidence, the touch of

derring-do he'd heard in it not five seconds ago having fled without a trace. "What…what are you doing down there?"

The question made him smile. "I'm here to help," he said softly. "If you need help, that is."

"I thought you'd left."

"Not yet. I was on the porch, waiting until the rain let up a little."

"Oh." Her pause continued into a slightly embarrassed hush. "You had an umbrella."

"Still do." He held it up for her to see if, indeed, she could make out the shape of a man and his umbrella in the shadows below. He had the advantage of the light from the window spilling down across her, illuminating the shimmery fabric of her slip, creating quite an interesting configuration of silhouette and womanly shape before it fell away, long before it could reach the shadows where he stood. "Is there a ladder somewhere nearby? That might help."

"No," she whispered back. "Monroe would be bound to hear you."

"Monroe being…"

"Our butler."

Peter nodded, wondering how Monroe had come to let the cat out on a night like this. "How are you planning to get down?"

"I usually go back in the way I came. Through the window."

Usually. As if she did this on a regular basis. "With the cat in your arms?" he asked.

"Tucked inside my shirt," she answered and then the embarrassed pause was back, as if she'd only just realized what she wasn't wearing. "Um, it's pretty dark out here, isn't it?"

"I can't even see my hands," he said, which was technically not a lie, as he wasn't looking at his hands and didn't intend to take his eyes off of Thea long enough to find out if they were, in fact, clearly visible. A raindrop plopped full on his cheek. "It's starting to rain again," he added, leery of her ability to get the cat and get back inside the house in a downpour. "Maybe I should try to get up to that window and come out to help you."

"No." Thea's whisper was fierce and determined. "I've almost got her now. Hold still, Ally..." She reached out—Peter saw the gleam of her skin as she leaned forward along the branch—but then, with a soft and startled, "Oh," she fell, tumbling down from her perch.

He barely had the presence of mind to step forward and catch her before she landed in his outstretched arms. They both hit the wet ground with a *splash,* a *thump,* a couple of *oomphs!* and a yowl of dismay from the cat, who clawed her way out of Thea's arms and climbed back up the tree as fast as she could scamper.

Chapter Four

The fall knocked the breath out of Thea and it felt like forever before she was able to suck in a deep, filling gasp of air. The very instant she did, however, she became wholly conscious that she was lying atop Peter Braddock. Full-length, front-to-front, face-to-face, and—Holy Cow!—he wasn't breathing. She pushed up, bracing herself with one hand on the ground while she pressed the other to his chest, pushing beneath his jacket, searching for the right place to check his heartbeat, hoping, *hoping,* she hadn't killed him.

"Peter?" she said, willing him to open his eyes. "Oh, please, don't be dead."

The rain beat down with renewed intensity, splashing through the tree leaves and striking her backside in a rhythmic tattoo that made it difficult to be sure the steady pulse beneath her palm was actually Peter's heartbeat. But then she felt his chest rise beneath her touch as he took several shallow breaths and a sweet, dizzy relief washed over her.

She stayed awash in that feeling right up until the

moment he opened his eyes and an electric awareness shot the relief to pieces and danced like fire from her heart to her toes then back again.

"So much...for proving...what a he-man...I am," he said between gasps. "I'd really planned...to catch you and...set you on your feet...not crumple...the minute you...landed."

"You broke my fall." His eyes at close range were a mesmerizing blend of greens and golds and Thea thought it might be possible to spend a century charting them all. "That was pretty brave."

His smile came slowly and, maybe just a tiny bit, pained. "Are you okay?"

She tested, flexing her ankles, her wrists, feeling the thrum of attraction everywhere her body touched his...which seemed to be an amazing number of places. "Yes," she said, still breathless from one thing or another. "Are you?"

He nodded. "It's still a little difficult to catch my breath, but other than that, I seem to be fine."

"I'm so sorry." She'd been so reckless to climb out after Ally, especially on a night like this, so careless to get caught out as she had, so stupid to fall out of the tree. "I could have killed you."

"I don't think so." His lips curved upward in a grin. "I'm made of pretty tough stuff...and you're a light-weight."

She realized she could have moved—*ought* already to have gotten off him—and a blush as warm as summer rose in a wave to her cheeks. "I'm sorry," she repeated. "No wonder you can't breathe." And she started to push away.

Peter's arms came around her, warm and strong and tight. "Don't be in such a hurry, Theadosia. Right now, you're the only thing keeping me from getting even wetter than I already am."

The blush curled down her neck, trickling with rising heat into her breasts. She was half-naked, scratched by the tree and the cat, soaked to the skin, chilled to the bone, and having very unladylike thoughts about the man she was lying upon. Not her usual modus oper-andi. Not even close...well, except for the scratched by the tree and the cat part. "I should go in," she said in a rush of shyness. "You should go home."

"I can't just yet."

"Oh, no, you *are* hurt."

"No, but your cat is back up in the tree."

She looked up, but Ally was long gone, probably farther up in the oak than she had been before. "Well, she can stay up there the rest of her life for all I care. I've saved her neck a dozen times and she's nearly cost me mine twice today already."

"Twice *today?*" His smile flashed with teasing good humor. "Did I see you out here earlier, Thea? Maybe just as I drove in to pick you up?"

"I don't see how you could have, Peter," she lied. "I was inside getting ready."

He grinned, still holding her against him. She had never been this close to him before. She wasn't sure she'd ever been this close to any man. She knew she'd never been this wet while being this close to anyone. Her slip clung to her like a second skin, and a thin skin at that. Maybe in this instance, being close to Peter was better than pulling away. The minute she moved away from him, he'd be able to see right through the wet silk and that would be more embarrassing even than this.

But not nearly so pleasant.

The thought deepened the heat in her cheeks. Between the cold rain falling on her backside and Peter using her as an umbrella, she could start sizzling at any second. Better to get up before something really humiliating happened. She pushed again against his chest and this time, he let her go.

"Thank you for breaking my fall." The words came out in a rush, as she tried to pull the clingy silk away from her body in the vain hope it would be less revealing. "Don't worry about the cat. She'll figure out how to get down sooner or later, I imagine."

"Apparently, she hasn't figured it out in the dozen or more times you've had to crawl out of your window to rescue her." He sat up, shrugging out of his sodden jacket, picking at the silk shirt which clung to his chest with a damp attention to detail.

Thea wished she looked half so good in her wet slip as he looked in his wet shirt. But he wasn't even looking at her and probably wouldn't notice if she took off every stitch of clothing she had on. Peter was a gentleman, and even if he hadn't been, he had no desire to look at her body, whether it was wet, dry or merely damp. She struggled to her feet, slipping a bit in the slick grass.

Peter caught her arm, helping her get her balance even as he got his feet under him and stood up. "You must be freezing," he said with a frown. "You've got goose bumps. Here, put on my jacket. It's wet, but maybe it'll provide a little bit of warmth."

There was something more going on than being cold, but Thea couldn't have told him what it was if she'd wanted to, so she pushed her arms through the sleeves of his jacket, which was very damp, but still provided some comforting warmth. And it smelled nice...like Peter's cologne. Or more aptly, like Peter's cologne in the rain. "I'd better go in now."

"Okay. I'll go with you."

"You w-will?"

"Well, if we can't get to the ladder without rousing the butler, I'll have to climb out your window to get to the cat."

Peter Braddock in her bedroom. Now there was a fantasy she'd never even allowed herself to imagine. Well, okay, so maybe she had thought about it once or twice when the moon was full and she was in a particularly daring mood. But in the flesh? She shivered at the idea of him stepping inside her room and seeing the private space where she lived and dreamed.

"Come on, Thea." He took hold of her arm, making the decision and turning her toward the front of the house. "You have to get in out of this rain before you catch pneumonia."

She gathered her wits enough to make a feeble protest at his choice of direction. "No, not the front. I go in through the kitchen. It's...closer." It was also safer, as it was a long way from her grandmother's rooms.

After two steps in the right direction, though, Thea stumbled, her bare feet slipping again on the wet grass.

"Put your arms around my neck," Peter said a second before he lifted her in his arms and settled her wet body against his wet chest.

Her heart started beating as fast as Ally's did when Thea held the kitten close after one of the tree-climbing incidents. It was a normal enough reaction, she thought. Any heart would have been startled at the events of the past few minutes. It probably had almost nothing to do with the fact that it was Peter who had picked her up and was now holding her, sheltered and snug in his arms. She hadn't expected him to carry her, didn't think it was necessary even now. But, oh, it felt nice to be held close, cradled so near a man's heartbeat.

"Keep your head tucked against my shoulder to keep the rain out of your face." Peter's breath was warm on her cheek, his voice soft and soothing in her ear. "I seem to have lost my umbrella."

"I'm sorry," Thea whispered, concerned now that he was regretting his chivalry. He had to be wishing he was anywhere but out in the rain with her. "There's one inside the house you can borrow."

He laughed. "I don't think an umbrella would do either of us much good at this point."

"I'm sorry," she said again…and he stopped short to look at her.

"Why are you apologizing?"

"Well, you're wet and…" How to let him know he didn't have to stay any longer? How to say, "you can go now," when it was the last thing she wanted him to do? "And well, you must be wishing you'd never agreed to…to go out with me tonight in the first place."

He held her while the rain splashed down over them and dripped from their hair and clothing. "I'm wet," he said finally, "because it's raining. And please believe me, Thea, not once tonight have I wished I could be anywhere else." His smile winged in, wiping away the very serious expression. "Well, that's not entirely true. Right now, I'm wishing rather fiercely to be somewhere it's not raining, but wet or dry, I'm not leaving Grace Place until I have you and your Ally cat safe and warm inside."

It was most likely all a lie, just his way of being tonight's hero and maybe gathering a story to tell to his brothers later, or to laugh over with any one of a dozen friends who'd never in a million years believe that he'd *wanted* to rescue her cat. Or her. It wasn't so much that she minded being the butt of jokes among the country club set, she just didn't want Peter to be the one doing the telling.

"So," he said briskly. "Do you think we could go inside now?"

She nodded, feeling oddly disloyal to Peter for even

thinking he was a liar, knowing in her heart that he had to be. "The door might be locked," she said when he started up the three steps to the kitchen door. "But there should be a key on the sill."

"That's the first place a burglar would look, you know."

"That's what Monroe says, but he leaves it there for me anyway...just in case."

Peter made it to the top of the steps where the overhang offered some protection from the rain before he set her on her feet and pulled back to look at her. "How often do you fall out of that tree, Thea?"

"Not often," she said and turned around, reaching up over the door to find the key, half-afraid she'd blurt out that the key on the sill was mostly wishful thinking on the part of Monroe and his wife, Sadie. Just a little inside joke between Thea and the household staff. "The key's really just for emergencies and we have an alarm system, so it's not as if a burglar would get very far if he found it."

"So what are the chances we'll set off the alarm as soon as we open the door? Not that I'm worried, you understand. I'd just like to be prepared."

Thea frowned, her fingers stretching, searching along the door sill. "We won't set off the alarm. I know the code."

"That's a point in our favor." He stepped closer to her on the narrow porch. "I'd really rather not have to explain to your grandmother why you're not in, uh, exactly the same shape you were when we left the house.''

"Believe me, Peter, it's in everyone's best interests if my grandmother never learns about this little escapade.''

"In that case, let me help.'' He reached above her easily, his chest pressing against her back, his arm brushing along her shoulder, his fingers moving over hers to investigate the sill.

Thea drew her hand down, going still as her whole body tensed with awareness. He was so male and she was, beneath it all, so very female, and nothing would ever in a million years come of this, but...*oh!* For the moment, it was like the delirium of a fever—all hot and bothersome and splendidly disconcerting.

He didn't seem to notice, although there was an instant—not longer than half a dozen rapid heartbeats—when Thea thought he must have felt the intensity of her attraction and recognized the desire permeating her entire being. And maybe, just for the time it took to breathe out and then in again, he felt something akin to awareness, too. It was probably nothing more than wishful thinking, but for someone like her, imagination was as close as she was ever likely to come to the real thing.

"Found it,'' he said and his body settled back into a normal position. His hands fell naturally to her shoulders, cupping the wet fabric of his coat, which was still wrapped around her, still enfolding her in his scent, still somehow keeping her teeth from chattering. "Now what do we do next?"

"I guess we open the door." She took the key he offered and peered doubtfully up at him through straggly wet strands of hair. "But really, Peter, you don't have to do this if you don't want to."

"I want to, Thea. Really." His smile came so easily, as if he meant what he said, as if he wasn't just being nice. "I hate to shatter your image of me, but it isn't every day that a woman literally drops out of the sky and into my arms. And believe it or not, I don't usually get to impress my date by climbing a tree and saving her cat. So, if it's all right with you, I'd sort of like to see what happens next."

She was reasonably sure that as soon as he saw her in the unforgiving light of a hundred-watt bulb, he'd come to his senses and beat a hasty retreat. But for now, all she could do was unlock the door and hope for the best.

"Sshhh." Thea put a finger to her lips, cautioning him to be quiet at the same time she motioned for him to follow.

As if he *wanted* to get caught sneaking up the back stairs to her bedroom.

Peter couldn't quite believe he was actually doing this, trailing after Thea like a shadow through the dimly lit hallways of Grace Place, wincing at the *squishy squish* sound his shoes made with every step, rehearsing excuses he could offer old Mrs. Carey if she happened to be waiting, like a horseman of the Apocalypse, at the top of the stairs.

Thea was taking it slowly, as if she was none too certain who or what might be waiting for them around the next dusky corner. She looked over her shoulder at him from time to time and Peter couldn't help thinking she was checking to see if he was still there. She was probably afraid he'd make a run for it, escape while he still had the chance. Or maybe her covert little glances stemmed simply from the novelty of taking a man up to her bedroom.

Of course, for all he knew, she could be in the habit of sneaking men upstairs every other night. Or even every night, for that matter.

But if Thea did entertain men in her room, she certainly hadn't gotten over being nervous about it. Or perhaps that was the thrill of it for her, the possibility of getting caught *en flagrante delicto*.

The idea of Thea conducting illicit trysts inside Grace Place was hard to imagine. Peter might not know a great deal about Thea's life, but he'd bet every car in the Braddock garage—even his grandfather's 1946 Rolls Royce classic—that he was the first man ever to be smuggled up through this narrow stairwell to the upper floors of the house. Okay, so he'd more or less invited himself to be smuggled inside, but if he hadn't, he was convinced she'd already be back out on that tree limb getting the dumb cat in out of the rain, and this time there'd be no man under the tree to break her fall.

The whole series of events still had him shaking his head. He'd always believed Thea had a story and he'd always known somehow that there was more to her than she allowed most people to see. As long as he could remember, she'd floated on the edge of his social group, an ethereal and strange little person, with her odd appearance and air of indifference, accepted because of her bluer than blue bloodlines, but never making any real effort to fit in, although never quite excluding herself from the circle, either.

Peter decided from now on he'd make more of an effort to draw her out and include her in any group of which he was a part. He might not be successful, but it couldn't hurt to try. He might even ask around, see if one of the lovely young women he knew might offer Thea some makeup tips or, at least, pass on the name of a reputable hairdresser.

It was possible, however, that hairdressers ran for cover at the mention of her name.

Peter had rarely seen anything look as bedraggled as Thea did at this very minute. *Bedraggled.* The one word perfectly described her appearance, although he now knew for a fact that she had hidden assets. At the moment, they weren't even well concealed. Even in the low light, he could see the sway of her hips beneath his jacket. Who could have guessed she had legs as long as a ballerina's and so precisely, exquisitely shaped?

He hadn't imagined the full and graceful curve of her breasts either, as she'd lain on top of him outside in the grass. He was even a trifle ashamed of himself for making the most of those few minutes of close contact. Probably he should have kept his focus on getting them both up off the wet ground as quickly as possible, but the opportunity had dropped into his hands and he was, after all, a thoroughly red-blooded American male. Noticing the shape and form of a woman came with the territory and so, well, he'd noticed.

He hadn't missed her shy, virginal blushes, either, or her awkward attempts to hide her attraction to him. Admittedly, there had been a couple of moments tonight when he'd responded to that attraction himself. It was a perfectly normal, natural thing to feel some shift toward arousal when in a somewhat compromising position with a member of the opposite sex. And in his defense, she was wearing only a silk slip.

A wet silk slip.

Peter stopped short, reminding himself it was *Thea* in that slip and he was on his way to her bedroom window to climb out on an oak limb and rescue a cat. Any other thoughts, any stray *Me, Tarzan, You, Jane* inclinations were not only out of line, but just plain ludicrous.

Thea stopped two steps above him and carefully, stealthily opened a door at the top of the stairwell. It creaked out a tiny whine that echoed past Peter and slipped into silence. Thea went absolutely still, then slowly leaned forward to peer around the door. His jacket rode up on her hips, as did the silk slip and Peter found himself with a view he'd never imagined he would have. His eyes followed the wickedly alluring line of trim ankles, shapely calves and slender thighs all the way up to…

Whoa, Nellie. He slammed his eyelids shut so fast he made himself dizzy and when he opened them again, he kept his gaze down, fixed on the shady outline of his water-stained, Italian-made shoes, distracting his attention with thoughts of anything other than Thea and the incredible view of her legs. The shoes were past saving, would no doubt have to be thrown out. *Thea was barefoot.* His slacks and the Armani shirt were probably ruined, too. *Why would she hide legs like that?* He plucked at the clammy silk shirt, suctioning it away from his rib cage with a pinch of his fingers, but it merely left one area of skin to cling to another. *She would look really terrific in a short, tight skirt.* He directed his thoughts away from that image and spent the next few seconds wishing he was on his way to a hot shower instead of another excursion into the rain.

He'd just save the cat and be on his way.

Here's your cat, ma'am. Glad to be of service.

In, out, on his way.

"Peter?"

Thea's whisper was as soft as a touch in the dark, and when he looked up, she was no longer in sight. But the door was open and he took the final steps quickly, stepping out into another dark hallway, bumping solidly into Thea, where she stood waiting for him.

He automatically reached out to steady her and as

his hand closed over her arm, he felt a lightning quick response snake through his body. "Sorry," he said, dropping the touch immediately, wondering what had gotten into him tonight. It had to be the element of clandestine excitement that had his blood pumping, had his adrenaline levels rocketing to his head, creating all manner of crazy thoughts and feelings and impulses…like pulling Thea into his arms and kissing her senseless.

Which was a prime example of why even a gentleman shouldn't be alone at midnight in the dark with a lady. Impulses could shoot out of nowhere and seem almost rational.

"This way." She brushed against him accidentally and the heat streaked up his arm again.

He inhaled a deep breath, gave his hand a vigorous shaking, and followed her to another door which, when opened, spilled a soft light over him and restored his sense of equilibrium.

"In here," she said and motioned him inside.

He stepped in and she swiftly closed the door behind him.

"This is my room."

As if he wouldn't have known. As if the bland walls and bare floors and odd-angled ceilings weren't a reflection of her. It was really a series of attic rooms, a jumble of open spaces and small cubicles cut up and integrated into one big living area. It was clean and neat, with a canopied bed covered in eyelet white with a motley, furry rug tossed across the foot. Peter stepped farther into the room, his architect's eye noting the artistic tilt of a screen divider; the symmetrical arrangement of a chest, a chair, an ottoman and a Tiffany floor lamp; the asymmetrical assortment of books and scattered sketchpads; the vivid color of autumn flowers tucked into niches all around.

"It's nice," he said. "Big."

"Yes." She ducked her head, her lank hair stringing forward onto her face, as if she was self-conscious about his presence in her bedroom.

Understandable, as he was feeling rather self-conscious about being here.

The rug at the foot of the bed stirred, sat up, and separated into four large cats. A black and white, a tabby, a tiger stripe and a gray. They yawned, stretched, licked their paws and eyed him consideringly.

"My cats," Thea said as she moved to the bed and scratched the gray under the chin.

"Cute," Peter said, not knowing much about cats or how to compliment them. "I take it, these four have more sense than to climb trees on nights like this one."

Thea rubbed the black and white's belly, the tabby's ear. "These four are older and have learned to stay out of trouble. I'm afraid Ally just isn't very smart."

She was smart enough to convince a twenty-something-year old woman to climb out and get her just to save her feline self the trouble of getting back into the house the same way she'd gotten out. But there was really no point in saying so. He followed the nip of cool, moist air to an open window and looked out at the thick limbs of the old oak. "Is this the way she gets out?" he asked.

"No, that's the way I get out. She's sneaky and slips out the door any time I'm not quick enough to catch her." Thea moved to the window, too and frowned out at the rainy darkness. "She then makes a beeline for my grandmother, who promptly tosses her calico butt outside. That's what I mean about Ally not being very smart. You'd think sheer survival instinct would keep her out of grandmother's way, but she'll go to her every time like a moth to a flame."

"Your grandmother doesn't like cats?"

"She detests animals of all kinds."

He nodded, not wanting to ask the obvious question.

With a sigh, Thea knelt by the window, rested her arms on the damp sill, laid her chin on her arms and answered the question he hadn't asked. "She tolerates me having pets because she knows I won't stay without them."

Which brought up the question of why she stayed here with her grandmother at all. But the rain wasn't slacking off much and the cat was still out in it and, if he wanted to be a hero—which he was no longer completely sure he did—he had to get on with it. "If you'll give me some room to get through the window, I'll see if I can get your cat for you."

She looked up at him, her hair limp and wet and stringy, her eyes brown and dark and deep, and said simply, "Thank you, Peter."

A strange tenderness clutched at his heart, confusing in its sweetness and out of place in the attic apartment. He replied with the only thought that came to mind. "What happened to your glasses?"

She blushed and looked away. "I don't...always wear them."

"I see." Which was a dumb thing to say. Better forget the small talk and just get the cat. "All right, here goes." He stuck one foot out the window, thought better of it, and pulled it back inside. "I think I'll do this without the shoes."

"Good idea."

He thought this was possibly the worst idea he'd had in quite some time. But there was no way he could say so now.

"You shouldn't do this," she voiced the thought for him and made it doubly impossible to back down. "Ally isn't your problem."

"I'm going after the cat," he said firmly. "Why don't you get some towels and dry yourself off while I'm out there? You must be freezing."

"I'm okay."

She was shivering. He could see that now he looked. His jacket hung on her and dripped a slow puddle from the hem and the cuffs. She was barefoot, standing in a steadily increasing pool of water, wet through and her lips had a slight blue tint. It didn't take a genius to see she needed to be dry and warm more than some silly cat. "Go into the bathroom, Thea." He placed his hands on her shoulders and turned her firmly away from the window. "Get out of those wet clothes and into the shower. Get warm. Get dry. By the time you come out, Ally and I will be back. Go." He urged her with an encouraging push.

"But you might need help," she protested, turning back. "What if you fall?"

"I'm not going to fall. Go, Thea."

She hesitated. "I'll wait until you're back inside."

"No, you won't." He took a step toward her. "Either you go get in the shower or I'll put you there myself. Your choice."

With a blink and another blush, she spun on bare heels and scurried off. Peter experienced a twinge of disappointment that she hadn't put up more of a fuss, but then if she had, where would he be? Backpedaling his way out of a meaningless threat, that's where. He was fairly certain putting a lady in a bathtub and turning on the shower was not on the list of things a gentleman should do.

So he slipped out of his sodden shoes, frowned at the cats lined up on the bed watching his every move, put his leg through the open window and made the small, but defiant, leap from the house onto the nearest oak branch.

THEA TURNED OFF the shower and stepped out of the tub, listening for Peter's voice calling for help. All she heard was the steady rhythm of the rain on the roof and the normal *drip…drip…drip…drip* of the showerhead. Grabbing a towel, she dried herself off, aided by a body temperature that rose alarmingly every time she thought about Peter Braddock in her bedroom. He could be right on the other side of the bathroom door. The idea sent a shiver of excitement through her naked body.

Or maybe she was just cold.

Or maybe Peter wasn't in the bedroom at all. Maybe he'd escaped while he had the chance.

Or maybe he was lying at the foot of the oak tree with a broken leg.

She hurriedly towel-dried her long, ropy hair, then scrubbed the terrycloth down her legs, swiped it across her back, over her hips, and pulled it once down the front. Now all she had to do was…dress.

She'd brought no clothes with her into the bathroom, too scattered by Peter's threat to put her in the shower himself to think that far ahead. So what to do? He might have fallen, might be waiting for her to notice he wasn't back and come to his aid. He might have gotten stuck in the tree—she knew it wasn't easy to get back through the window with a struggling kitten in hand. He might need the ladder. Or an ambulance.

Deciding this was no time to be squeamish over showing a little skin—and it wasn't as if she'd been decently dressed when she fell on top of him, or since—Thea wrapped the towel around her and opened the door. "Oh." The sight of Peter, sitting on the windowsill, a lot wetter even than he'd been before holding a scraggly, unhappy kitten in his arms, startled the word right out of her. "You made it."

He looked up and a raindrop rolled down his cheek, dropped off his chin onto the cat, who mewed in devout misery. "Don't sound so surprised," he said. "Although, you might have warned me that your Ally cat would be somewhat averse to being rescued."

Thea forgot about her lack of clothes, forgot about the way she looked, forgot that she was coming fresh from the shower to the feet of a man who shouldn't be in her bedroom, even in her fantasies. Stooping in front of him, she touched his sodden shirt, saw the pulled threads, the scratches on his neck, the beaded evidence of blood on his hands. "She scratched you. I'm so sorry."

"To be fair, I probably scared her out of a good three lives out there." He gently stroked the top of the cat's wet head. "I think she was expecting you and when I grabbed her, she went kind of wild for a minute."

Thea didn't know what to say, how to properly thank him. So she just took Ally out of his hands and cuddled the soggy ball of fur against her towel-covered breast as she offered Peter an apologetic gaze. "You're nearly as soaked as she is."

He looked down at the puddle spreading under him, then lifted his shoulder in a wry shrug. "Maybe you could bring me a towel?"

She nodded, stood, started to comply, stopped. "Why don't you just hop in the shower and warm up a little bit? You can't go home like this."

"I don't think I have much of a choice, Thea."

"I have a hair dryer," she said, eager to do something, anything to help. "I'll blow some of the moisture out of your clothes while you shower. That way, at least, you won't get your car all wet."

"You could let me borrow a towel to put on the seat."

"I don't have that many towels. I'll just get the hair dryer and then the bathroom's all yours."

"Thea, I'll shower when I get home." But she didn't listen, just carried Ally with her into the bathroom, wondering as she went what would happen if she threatened him as he had threatened her. What a silly thought. Nothing would happen. Except he'd probably laugh at her for making an idle, impossible-to-carry-out threat and she'd be embarrassed anew. As if she could force Peter into her shower. As if she had the courage to even say such a thing to him. As if she wouldn't be overcome with shyness at the mere thought of him undressing in her bathroom.

But he couldn't go home soaked to the skin like he was. If he died of some horrible weather-related illness, she'd never forgive herself.

"Okay," she said coming out of the bathroom with the hair dryer and walking straight to the bed. "The bathroom's all yours. Just open the door and put your clothes out when you're ready and I'll work on drying the worst of the rain out of them while you shower."

She could hardly believe the words came out so easily, as if she sent men in to shower every day of the week. "I laid out a couple of towels for you and there's shampoo and soap and…everything." The heat scalded her cheeks, but she didn't look at Peter, didn't take the chance of seeing him appalled by the thought of sharing her shampoo, her soap...the towels she used.

"I don't think this is a good idea, Thea." But he stood up, still dripping. "What if...someone...comes to the door?"

She risked a glance at him and decided he was the handsomest man she'd ever seen soaking wet. Of course, as he was the *only* man she'd ever seen soaking wet, she supposed being the handsomest wasn't a particularly great honor. "My grandmother never comes to my room, Peter. Ever. No one comes to my room."

He looked like he was going to protest, or say he was sorry or something equally dreadful, so she bent down to plug in the hair dryer cord. And the next thing she heard was the sound of his footsteps as he crossed the room, followed by the closing of the bathroom door.

The cat mewed in her arms and Thea set her down on the bed, shooing away Ally's curious friends by turning on the dryer and giving the shivering kitten a quick blow-dry. She didn't hear the bathroom door open again, but when she went to gather Peter's clothes, they were in a soggy pile outside and the shower was running full-blast. Lifting the topmost piece of clothing—his slacks—she carried them to the bed and draped them loosely across the footboard. Then she straightened the cord, turned the dryer on high, and aimed the heated air at the pants.

The blast of heat steamed up around her and she

tried to concentrate, tried *not* to think about Peter, using her shower...her soap...her shampoo. But she knew she'd never be able to step into her own shower again without imagining him there, without remembering how she'd dried his clothes while he was naked just on the other side of that door. Nothing had happened. Nothing had even come close to happening, but she knew that for many nights to come, she'd fall asleep in her bed with the memory of how it had felt to be held close in his arms, how it felt to imagine him in her shower—in her bed.

And when she was alone, she would admit that it had felt good. Unbelievably good.

Of course, she'd never tell him that. She'd never even let on that she remembered. She wouldn't want to do or say anything to embarrass him and, even as kind as Peter was, she knew he would be embarrassed later when...*if*...he recalled their first and only date. So she'd keep the memory to herself, take it out like a treasure when she was lonely or blue, smile to herself at the thought of him climbing out the window in the rain to rescue her silly cat.

The cord tangled and, when she reached down to straighten it out again, the towel slipped and Thea barely caught it before it fell. Silly cat, indeed. What was her excuse for piddling around, drying his clothes, when it hadn't even once occurred to her she needed to put on clothes, herself? Knotting the towel back in place, she turned off the hair dryer and set it on the floor.

She'd taken only two hurried steps toward the closet, though, when the bathroom door opened and Peter looked out. Steam wisped out around him and he fanned the door a little, revealing a towel wrapped around his waist and glimpses of his damp, hairy chest and the scratches Ally had made across his shoulders and neck.

"How's it coming?" he asked, smiling easily, as if they weren't both half-naked and pretending they weren't.

"I was just going to get..."

Thea felt a puff of air and looked toward the window, to make sure it was closed.

It was.

But the door to her bedroom was not.

Davinia Carey stood there, like a wrathful god, her white hair contrasting with the severe black dressing gown she wore like a judge's robes, her eyes as cold and hard as granite as they took in the scene.

Thea's heart jerked and dropped like a rock.

Behind her, she heard Peter step out to stand with her and wished with all her being, she could find the courage to shield him from her grandmother's great displeasure.

But she knew already it was too late to save him.

And she was years too late to save herself.

Chapter Five

Archer entered the library, depending a little more than usual on the support of his cane. Three heads lifted as he walked into the room, three faces tried—and failed—to mask their low spirits. He sought Peter's gaze first, but the green eyes, so like his own, so like James's, turned away after the barest touch of a glance. Embarrassed. Archer didn't know what he could say to make his grandson understand he wasn't disappointed in him. If anything, this whole sorry mess had shown what a strong character Peter truly possessed.

"Dad?" James stood, a dozen questions threaded through the single word.

"May I get you something to drink, Archer?" Ilsa stood, too, overly anxious to help, feeling guilty over something that hadn't been her fault, worrying over consequences that had never been in her power to prevent.

"Thank you," Archer said and moved to sit in his favorite chair, one nearest the fire. "A little brandy would be nice."

He used the cane for support, until he was settled into the comfortable cushions of the wingback chair, then he hooked the curved handle of the cane on the arm of the chair and leaned his head against the tapestried seatback. He looked again at Peter, but got only a hesitant response, another cutaway glance, the brief flicker of a strained smile.

"Here you go." Ilsa handed him a glass with just enough brandy to coat the bottom a deep, rich gold.

It wasn't much liquor, but for a man his age it would be plenty to coat his belly with warmth and lend him a bit of courage. The next few minutes doubtless would not hold much pleasure for any of them. "Thank you, my dear." Archer took a sip of the liquor and cupped the glass between his palms before he looked at each of them in turn. James still showed the tense jaw and narrowed brow of anger; Ilsa's lovely face reflected the worry of a friend who badly wants to set things aright; Peter wore the defeated look of a young man determined to do the right thing no matter the personal cost. "I've been with Davinia," Archer said, although they all knew full well where he'd been and why. "Miles Jordan, her lawyer, was present most all of that time and we—"

"Lawyer?" James bit out the word as if it left a bad taste in his mouth. "Don't tell me that crazy old woman thinks she can sue us over this."

Archer cautioned James with a mere lift of his brow. "Her lawyer was there because she plans to change her will."

Peter looked up, met Archer's eyes. "She's going to cut Thea out of her inheritance, isn't she?"

At Archer's nod, Peter got up and paced restlessly to the north window. He was taking this too personally, Archer felt, but in two days no one had been able to convince him he was not to blame.

"So what?" James stated the words Archer had thought himself at first. So what if Thea didn't inherit anything from her grandmother? She had money from her father's estate, money from her half brother's estate, money from the Berenson chain of jewelry stores. "She doesn't need the Grace fortune," James continued. "Elizabeth Carey married Berenson to get out from under her mother's thumb. She would have seen to it that her child's future didn't depend on the whims of that old harridan."

"Her name is Davinia Carey," Archer said. "She may be old and we may not agree with her moralistic views, but she is not crazy and in this household at least, we will continue to speak of her with respect."

"I don't see why. She's accused Peter of everything from lying to her face to taking advantage of her granddaughter, to ruining the girl's life. She first demands an apology, then refuses to allow Peter to make one, even though I see no reason he should apologize to her or anyone else. She's cloistered Thea away as if this was Victorian England, not America in the twenty-first century and then she commanded you, Dad, to appear before her this afternoon to explain why you're not as outraged as she is. Frankly, I don't think the woman gives a damn if we *respect* her or not.''

Archer swirled the brandy in his glass, wondering if he and Jane would have been better parents to their only child had they been a little less strict, a lot more relaxed and a bit more respectful of his right to his own opinions. Perhaps had they known the tremendous losses James would suffer early in adulthood—the loss of Lily, his first love, then only a few years later, Mariah, his second wife, and then Catherine, Peter's mother—maybe they would have loved him a little more and expected a little less. He and Jane had done better in parenting their three grandsons. But Archer believed James was a good man. There was no doubt he loved his sons and was trying to make amends for his failure to be a good father when they were young. Still he was too quick to anger, too hasty in taking offense, too eager to go on the defensive here, instead of allowing Peter to choose his own battles. ''We will be respectful, James, because we are gentlemen and because to do anything less is not only a poor reflection on this family, but also nonproductive.''

''Did you see Thea?'' Peter asked, maintaining his observation of the gardens beyond the library windows.

''For a moment.'' Archer sighed, acknowledging at least to himself, that in some ways Davinia was inexcusably and rigidly old-fashioned. ''She tried to give me a message for you, but she was…interrupted.''

Peter looked back at Archer. ''A message?''

''I believe she wanted me to tell you she's sorry.''

Peter's jaw flexed with his tension. "Do you think Mrs. Carey would allow me to talk to Thea?"

James made a scoffing sound. "Give it up, Peter. She's made it clear she doesn't want you to step foot on her property ever again or make any attempt to contact Thea at any time in the future. I believe the old bat…excuse me, I mean, *Mrs. Carey*…has formed the outrageous opinion that you're not good enough for her granddaughter."

Archer caught the flicker of doubt in Peter's eyes and wished James had not made that particular point. For a moment, too, he was angrier with Davinia Carey than James could ever be. But anger would not resolve this situation, nor would it help Peter accept that he *was* good enough for Thea. For James. For any and all of the people he still believed judged him for his illegitimate past rather than his legitimate present.

"I want to talk to her. Thea." Peter looked from Archer to Ilsa. "Can you arrange something, Mrs. Fairchild?"

Ilsa wanted to help. It was written all over her face. "I don't know, Peter," she said. "I can try."

Peter nodded, understanding the subtle nuances of dealing with a woman like Davinia Carey. Archer was proud of him for that. Like it or not, there were rules they all had to play by. Whether they agreed with the rules was unimportant. It was simply the way their world worked. "Thank you," Peter said and turned back to contemplating the garden and who knew what multitude of imagined sins. Peter had come into the family already wounded by life. He was still too ready to believe that was somehow his fault.

"Peter?" Archer reclaimed his grandson's attention, even though he did not want to say what had to be said next. He was afraid Peter would take it as a personal challenge and not as simply the best and only way to proceed. "I believe we've done all we can. Davinia lives by an outdated and rather outlandish set of principles. She has chosen to believe the worst of both you and Thea, no matter who tells her otherwise. That's unfortunate for Thea, as she obviously is distressed to have disappointed her grandmother and to have involved you. However, you've tried to explain, you've offered an apology for your part of the misunderstanding. I think this has to be an end to it. Especially considering you didn't do anything wrong in the first place. There just isn't anything more to be done. Thea will have to deal with her grandmother on her own now."

There was no discernible change in Peter's stance, but the hands he held clasped loosely at his back clenched and released...and clenched again. Archer knew what that meant. Peter wasn't through with Davinia Carey.

Maybe if he had said the words differently...but Archer had learned over the years he wasn't responsible for someone else's choice. Peter had to choose for himself and learn the lessons those choices held for him. But that didn't stop Archer from wishing devoutly that he'd never asked Peter to take Thea out on Saturday or any other time. Blame was pointless, though, in this case, where one person had so much influence over another. Davinia wielded considerable power over her granddaughter and now, consequently, over Peter.

Archer tapped the snifter with a finger gnarled by age and arthritis, and decided he shouldn't withhold the rest of the information he had learned this afternoon at Grace Place, either. "It does appear that Davinia has managed over the years to tie up all of Thea's assets in a trust which cannot be breached until she's of age…in this case, not a day before her thirtieth birthday."

"That's ridiculous," James said, ready to tackle Davinia Carey from another angle. "A good attorney could pierce that clause without half trying."

"You may be right." Archer raised the brandy to his lips and let the liquor warm his throat again. "But for that to happen Thea would have to consult a good attorney and I can't see her defying her grandmother in that way."

Ilsa leaned forward in her chair. "But, Archer, you're talking almost as if Thea was a minor child. She's twenty-five and, even if she doesn't want to challenge the trust, she must have other options."

Archer inclined his head. "Perhaps. But we can't discount the fact that Davinia is the only family Thea has, the only family the child has ever known. Berenson died young. Elizabeth, too. The half brother was nearly two decades older than Thea and I don't believe she had much contact with him, even before his death. It's unfortunate for Thea that Davinia is such a strong personality and that she puts such pride in her ancestry and heritage. She has always had very definite ideas about what society expects of a lady of wealth and position, although she didn't used to be quite so implacable and stubborn. She nearly went mad with grief when Elizabeth died, but then there was Thea, and a second chance at raising a child. While it's true that in our opinion, she simply went from one extreme to another, I'm sure in her mind she is protecting Thea from the excesses which killed Elizabeth."

"Not everyone would agree it was *excess* that killed Elizabeth." James walked to the fireplace and stirred the fire. "I'm sorry, Dad," he said after a moment. "I'm just angry she's made such a fuss and stirred up a tempest out of nothing. She's acted as if Thea and Peter are adolescents and not responsible young adults. What they do in or out of their bedrooms is none of our business, and that should go double for Davinia Carey."

"You're quite right, James." Ilsa's soft assurance had a soothing affect, Archer could tell, and it pleased him to see his son respond to a woman with good sense, for a change. In the past several years, James hadn't exactly chosen his love interests for their intellect and understanding. Now, however, it was beginning to look as if he'd come to his senses and realized what he'd been missing. "However," Ilsa continued. "She has made it our business—well, at least, your business—because she contacted Archer to apprise him of what had happened and to demand that he present himself at Grace Place today to discuss what should be done." Ilsa glanced at Archer. "I do hope you managed at some time this afternoon to persuade her this should remain a *private* matter."

Archer smiled without humor. "Believe me, if this little contretemps leaks out, it won't have come from Grace Place."

"What would happen to the trust if Thea marries?" Peter asked suddenly.

"Marries?" James repeated. "I don't think that's a realistic option for her, Peter. I imagine Davinia would have taken steps to safeguard the trust against fortune-hunters and, while it isn't a particularly tactful point to make, who else would marry Thea?"

The air fairly snapped to attention, jabbing the chilly finger of alarm right through Archer and piercing the warm glow of the brandy, as Peter turned from the window, his chin up, his eyes fierce in their determination.

"I would," he said calmly. "In fact, marrying Thea is exactly what I intend to do."

LEAVING THE LIBRARY before the shocked and satisfying silence could come to a rolling boil, Peter took the stairs two at a time. At the top of the first landing, he paused, then did something he hadn't done in years. He jumped and high-fived the portrait of old Josiah Braddock. Well, in truth, he barely touched the ornate gold frame next to old Joe's hands—Grandmother would have had a fit if any of them had ever actually laid a finger on the portrait. She had used to complain that her grandsons' high spirits would be the death of her, but in the end she'd succumbed only to a heart worn out from happiness and a good long life.

Peter had taken his own sweet time after coming to live at Braddock Hall to observe his two older brothers. It had taken a good long while after that to work up the courage to try the high-five jump, even though he'd watched Adam and Bryce do it on almost every charge up the staircase. Touching that picture frame had been one of the coveted goals of his adolescence, and the day he'd finally grown tall enough and could jump high enough to high-five old Joe, had been one of the best days of his life.

A little like he felt today…proud of himself in a way he couldn't have fully explained.

Marrying Thea is exactly what I intend to do.

He could hardly believe he'd even conceived the thought, much less voiced it aloud. But there it was.

In a few minutes, he figured James would be coming after him, wanting to know what maggot of insanity had bypassed his brain and come straight out of his mouth. Already, Peter could hear the rumble of voices…his dad's edgier, rougher and more demanding than the other two, Archer's reasoned response, Ilsa's reassuring contralto. He wondered what they were saying, if they'd believed him, if they thought he'd simply been making a bad joke.

But it wasn't a joke. Not at all. He'd been thinking the only way to get Thea away from her grandmother was going to be for someone to marry her when James had asked the question.

Who else would marry her?

Who, other than a man only interested in her money, would marry poor, ugly-duckling Theadosia Berenson?

And suddenly, Peter couldn't bear the thought of Thea married to some ne'er-do-well with sunbleached hair, capped teeth, breezy manners, expensive habits and a taste for extramarital affairs. Someone who'd push her further into the background, further into herself and humiliate her in ways she'd never be able to defend against. In the long run, a marriage like that would be far worse for her than her present relationship with her hateful and domineering old grandmother.

Not that he wanted to marry Thea.

He didn't want to marry anyone. Not for years and years.

But someone had to rescue her. She was locked up in the attic rooms of Grace Place as surely as if someone turned the key in the door every night. She was confined in the world her grandmother had created to keep her safe. Maybe his grandfather was right in his assessment of Davinia Carey. Maybe she was, in her way, only trying to keep Thea from repeating the mistakes her mother had made. Maybe she was simply protecting Thea as best she knew how. But whatever her motives, Mrs. Carey had only trapped Thea into a belief system that was neither healthy nor true. And being a gentle soul, Thea had come to believe she could not, should not even wish, to escape.

Peter knew how someone like Thea could come to think she had no other options. Hadn't he watched his mother do exactly that in her own life? Hadn't she convinced herself that in order to escape a bad and abusive marriage, she would have to sacrifice one or the other of her children? And in the end, hadn't she died rather than make such a terrible choice? Peter had been angry about that for a long time. Angry with James for not rescuing all three of them. Angry with Catherine for not being brave enough to save herself and consequently, both him and Briana, his half sister. But most of all, Peter had been angry that *he* hadn't done something, anything at all, to ransom them from his mother's strong, but mistaken beliefs.

He took the remaining stairs at a pensive pace, thinking about Thea living in the attic room with cats for company and flowers for color with only an embittered and narrow-minded grandmother to love her. Growing up in that household with its cold, dark hallways and cold, critical air, it was a miracle Thea had a heart at all.

But she had a sweet and tender heart. He'd always known that, somehow. Just as he'd always thought that someone within their social circle ought to, and would eventually, do something to help her.

Saturday night had changed his thinking on that. *He* was that nebulous someone. *He* had to do something. Right or wrong, he could no longer pretend there was someone else to do it. Saving Thea might not be the best way of rewriting his own history, but he felt responsible and as if he'd burst if he didn't at least try to talk to her. After that...well, if the only idea he could come up with to get her away from Grace Place was to marry her, then that's what he'd do. Crazy idea or not.

He wondered what his Grandmother Jane would say about it. She'd always reminded him to follow his heart, although this probably wasn't exactly what she'd meant. Still, it felt like the right thing to do. His mother had always told him he must make his life count, that he was born to be a gentleman and that it was his responsibility in life to make certain he died a gentleman. "You're a Braddock," had been the end of every bedtime story he'd ever heard until he was nine and learned his mother hadn't made up the stories she'd told him. When she died, he'd found out in a hurry that *Braddock* wasn't just Catherine's way of describing a chivalrous code of behavior, that *Braddock* was not a strange synonym for gentleman or another way of reminding him to be a good boy. Braddock was, in fact, the name of a family. *His* name, as it turned out, and *his* family. Although he'd really had very little understanding of what that meant, at the time.

When he reached his room, Peter went immediately to pick up the only picture he had of his mother. It was a snapshot, a close-up, taken at the beach some long ago summer. She was wearing a beach hat, holding it on with one hand while the wind tugged at her hair beneath the wide, sun-shading brim, and laughing at the camera as if she had not a care in the world. Peter liked to think even if he'd had dozens of pictures of Catherine to choose from that this would be the one he'd want to remember her by.

"She was a beautiful woman," James said from the doorway. "Your mother."

Peter nodded and set the picture in its silver frame back on the chest of drawers. "I was just thinking about her," he said. "Wishing her life might have been different."

"There's hardly a day that goes by I don't think about her and wish...well, so many things." James leaned a shoulder against the dark wood of the doorjamb. "I wonder how all of our lives might have been different had she told me in the beginning that she was married. Or if later she'd mentioned Briana. Or if she'd only known she was pregnant with you when she left to go back to him. But none of those things happened. She chose what she chose, Peter."

He knew it was true, had long since absorbed and accepted Grandmother Jane's philosophy that assigning blame could only cloud the present without changing one single moment of the past. He did believe James hadn't known about Catherine being already married when they'd met. And not until she died, about their son. "I know." Turning away from his mother's picture, he began unbuttoning his shirt. "But I don't think you came up here to talk about my mother."

"No, although there are times when I think every conversation you and I have ever had is about her." He paused, straightened and drew away from the door, offered a hopeful smile. "What you said downstairs just now, Peter...you're just angry, right?"

Peter shrugged out of his shirt. "I am angry, Dad, yes." He walked to the closet and stepped inside, looking for another shirt, something suitable to wear while paying a call on a lady.

"Good, because I'd hate for you to think marriage is the answer."

Peter came out of the closet, pulling on the shirt he'd chosen—a pale blue stripe.

"And believe me," James continued. "I know what you're thinking—I'm the last person in the world to be giving advice about who you should or shouldn't marry."

"That's not what I'm thinking, Dad. I'm thinking I want to see Thea and talk to her."

"Don't ask for trouble, Peter. Davinia Carey doesn't want you anywhere near her granddaughter. At least not now. Give this some time. Believe me, trying to talk to Thea right now is not a good idea."

"I appreciate the warning, Dad." Peter finished buttoning the blue-striped shirt, feeling—as he sometimes did with James—more like the adult in their relationship than the child. "But I need to talk to Thea and I'm afraid it can't wait for a better time."

James frowned, obviously anxious to say something to deter his son from making a big mistake. "Peter, stop and think about this. No matter what went on in that bedroom the other night, marrying Thea is not the answer."

"I believe you." Peter reached into the closet for his leather jacket. The rain on Saturday had left the outside air with a wintry crispness. "Don't wait dinner for me tonight. This may take a while."

"She's a crazy old woman and she could shoot you on sight," James said as Peter walked past him and out into the hall. "Which, come to think of it, might actually bring you to your senses."

"It might," Peter agreed cheerfully as he headed for the stairs. "But I doubt it."

"STOP FIDGETING, THEA, and eat your dinner." Davinia put down her fork and frowned at the untouched food on Thea's plate. "I have no intention of allowing you to make yourself sick over this." She nodded at the food. "Now eat."

"I'm not hungry." Thea saw no reason to choke down food she had neither asked for nor wanted. Besides, if she swallowed so much as a morsel, she knew her stomach would toss it right back up.

"Don't be missish. I told you I spoke with Archer Braddock this afternoon and, while he wasn't as shocked as he should have been, he has assured me that his grandson will not bother you again. We can forget this unfortunate incident happened and get back to normal around here."

Normal, Thea thought. As if that was a good thing. As if normal had so much to offer. "Grandmother, nothing happened. Your talking to Mr. Braddock about it only makes it seem like something did."

"I am not stupid, Theadosia. I saw exactly what was going on with my own eyes and right under my own roof. Frankly, the more you protest, the more convinced I am that you're becoming as untrustworthy as your mother."

"But Grandmother, nothing..."

Davinia held up a hand, the scowl she had worn continuously for two days intensifying. "We will not discuss this any further, Theadosia. I believe I have made my views quite clear on the subject and I consider the matter closed. You made a mistake by allowing that young man to talk his way into your bedroom, but I am willing to share some small part of the responsibility. I went completely against my own better judgment in allowing you to go out with him in the first place. While I have tremendous regard for Archer Braddock—which is the only reason I accepted his suggestion that Peter should be your escort on this occasion—I knew I should not have agreed. Peter may be a Braddock, but that whole scandal with his mother and the horrible man she was married to never rang quite true with me. There's bad blood in Peter Braddock. You mark my words."

"But, Grandmother..." Thea felt she owed it to Peter to at least try and defend him. But as had happened the other night, her words fell into the wake of Davinia's suppositions and were ignored.

"Rest assured, Thea, I will be much more selective in choosing your escorts in the future."

As if young men were lined up around the block

waiting to ask her out. As if she wouldn't have enough sense to choose a good one if they were.

"Now," Davinia continued briskly, "eat your dinner. Sadie went to a deal of trouble to prepare some of your favorite dishes. The least you can do is be appreciative of her hard work and eat what has been set in front of you."

Thea signed and picked up her fork. She could protest until she turned blue and she'd still never be able to generate the same passion, the same absolute authority that her version was, in fact, the truth. And although Thea didn't think Sadie would be offended if she sent her plate back to the kitchen as full as it had come out, she didn't want to risk making anyone else mad at her. It was easier to pretend to eat. Grandmother wasn't one to turn a blind eye, whether it was how much food was eaten or what she had seen in Thea's bedroom only two nights ago.

And what she'd seen was Peter Braddock, fresh from the shower, and unbearably, beautifully, bare. Well, except for the towel. But Thea had thought that only added to the charm, the utter mystery of being alone with a man in her bedroom. She'd hadn't, of course, had much time to enjoy the charm or solve any of the mystery. Not that there had ever been any chance she would. Peter wasn't interested in her. Never had been. Never would be.

Which only meant she was sick to her soul over the scene her grandmother had made in front of him.

Of *course*, he wouldn't bother her again.

He had every reason to stay as far away from her as humanly possible. No more duty dances. No more of his gentle teasing. No more moments when she felt almost as if he understood. She doubted she'd even catch a glimmer of his smile after this. And no one would think any less of him for it, either. She could imagine the gossip that could already be circulating.

Thea's always had a crush on Peter.

She probably threw herself at him.

How embarrassing for him.

And after he'd been kind enough to take the poor thing to Angela's wedding, too. Then to take her home and have her grandmother act as if he'd planned a seduction all along.

How awful that must have been.

But he's such a gentleman, you know. I can't imagine he'd have told Davinia Carey straight out that he'd have to be utterly desperate to even think about seducing her granddaughter. Thea? Teddy Bear Berenson? Can you imagine?

There'd be laughter then, Thea imagined. Because, of course, Peter was young, handsome, rich and so far from *utterly* desperate, even she could see the humor in such a statement.

Grandmother never saw much humor in anything though. She lived in fear Thea would become just like Elizabeth. Wild, reckless, irresponsible and…dead. It did no good for Thea to assure her that she was none of those things and had no inclination to follow in her mother's impetuous footsteps. It was a settled thing in

Davinia's mind. Thea had inherited a streak of self-destructive and impulsive behavior and, sooner or later, if the proper precautions weren't taken, it would show itself. *Had* shown itself, in fact, on Saturday night.

Davinia paused in the enjoyment of her dinner to check Thea's progress with hers. Apparently satisfied, she raised her glass and sipped her wine. "This week, Thea, I think you must get out and about a little more than usual. And I'm not referring to your early morning jaunts to the beaches to sketch, either. Nor do I mean you should spend more time volunteering at that Thrift Shop where you are far too generous with your time and talent as it is. I want you to be seen at social gatherings. I want your head held high. I want a smile on your face. A lady of quality transcends petty gossip and if, as I fear, word of Saturday's tête-à-tête gets out, we will have gone a long way to refute it by having you seen about as if nothing happened."

"Nothing *did* happen," Thea said.

"Yes, that's best. Say that, in just that way, Thea, should anyone be rude enough to hint around at asking. I don't believe anyone will dare to be so rude to my granddaughter, but just in case, it's always better to be prepared."

Thea sometimes thought her life had been one long preparation for *just in case*. Davinia spent a considerable amount of her days reasoning out every possible trap a lady might face and a strategy against it, then preparing Thea for the worst. As if the worst hadn't happened, anyway. As if she hadn't grown up with the constant fear of making a mistake, of saying the wrong thing at the wrong time, of doing something wrong, of doing *anything* at all. As if she hadn't learned it was safest to say nothing at all, to stay in the background and draw as little attention to herself as possible.

Thea sighed and stopped pretending to eat. "You said you didn't believe there would be any gossip," she said.

Davinia looked at her sadly. "I imagine young Braddock will boast of your indiscretion, Thea. Men like him always do."

Thea believed it was much more likely to leak out because of all the horrified whisperings and hush-hush discussions Davinia had held behind closed doors. With her attorney, Miles Jordan, with Monroe and Sadie, with Archer Braddock. There was nothing more conducive to spreading something one didn't wish to spread than conducting private meetings about the matter. Thea wouldn't, of course, say that any of the principal players would gossip, but she believed at least one of them would slip and say something to someone who would, in turn, pass it on to someone else. One heedless whisper was all it took to form a scandal. The world was still a very small place in that way.

But the one thing Thea did know for certain is that whatever form the gossip took, it wouldn't originate with Peter.

"Peter won't breathe a word of this," she told her grandmother with certainty. "Regardless of what you think of him, he's a gentleman and he's always been very kind to me.''

Davinia nodded, her eyebrows arched by both nature and artistry. ''It's the *kind* men you must be on our guard against, Theadosia. As you found out the other night. But now, let's talk of something more pleasant. A trip, perhaps. What would you think of going...''

Far off, the doorbell chimed, a great well of echoing chords, fading away almost before it could reach them there in the dining room and taking with it whatever more pleasant topic Davinia had been about to introduce. No one was expected and no one ever came to Grace Place unexpectedly, so the ringing of the doorbell was a mystifying interruption. Thea took the opportunity to cover her plate with the linen napkin, covering up the evidence, hoping she'd be safely in her room before her grandmother realized she'd only pushed food around and hadn't eaten a bite.

''A visitor, Madam,'' Monroe announced from the doorway some few moments later, his kind old eyes cutting to Thea with subtle warning. ''For Miss Theadosia.''

''Who is it, Monroe?'' Thea pushed back her chair, eager for any excuse to escape.

''*Sit down,* Thea.'' Davinia patted her napkin to her lips. ''Miss Theadosia is at dinner, Monroe, and if you'll recall, I believe I informed you earlier that she would not be at home for visitors until further notice.''

As if Monroe was accustomed to turning away

Thea's friends in droves. As if she had friends who would drop by at dinnertime...or any other time.

"It's Mr. Braddock," Monroe said with another meaningful glance at Thea. "Mr. Peter Braddock."

Thea was out of her chair like a shot, determined to see Peter and apologize for the horrible things her grandmother had said to him and about him, even if it meant she had to spend the rest of her life in her room.

"Thea!"

But she dashed past the butler and out of the room as if the hounds of hell were on her heels. And one of them soon would be. "Peter?" she called softly, breathless with the exertion and the idea that he had come. Like a gallant knight in a fairy tale. Like a man who knew just how desperately she needed a friend. "Peter?"

He was in the entry hall, shadowed in the gloom, wearing a soft blue shirt with stripes. Well, she thought it was striped. How could anyone notice a shirt when he was in it? And she didn't care if he had come in a suit of armor or with a legal order to cease and desist. She just cared that he had come. No matter what his reason. "Peter," she said, smiling just a little, nervous and thrilled and anxious all at the same instant. "Hi."

He smiled, tightly, as if he were a little nervous, too. And after Saturday night...well, he was very brave to come here. "Are you all right?" he asked.

As if it mattered. As if he was concerned. As if she might not be. "Yes," she said simply. "Are you?"

He nodded and she jumped into her apology. "I'm so sorry, Peter. It was awful for you and I can't believe it happened and I'd give anything if it hadn't, but she never comes to my room. Ever. I don't know what horrid trick of fate made her climb the stairs and—"

"Thea!"

Peter stepped forward, touched her hand. "I need to know if you're really all right, Thea. I need to know because—"

"Young man, you will take your hand off of my granddaughter and leave my house this instant." Davinia walked into the foyer, tall, straight and forbidding. "I do not wish to have to involve the police because of my respect for your grandfather, but make no mistake about it, I will if you make it necessary. And I will press charges. Don't think I won't." She made a gesture with one thin hand, motioning toward where Monroe hovered behind her, ready presumably to make the call if she so directed. "Shall we phone the authorities or will you leave without a fuss?"

"Mrs. Carey," Peter said, his voice as solid as steel in the big, dusky hall. "I'm here to talk to Thea. Alone."

"I think not." Davinia didn't budge from her position or from her decree. "My granddaughter is not interested in anything you have to say. Not now or at any time in the future."

"Thea?" Peter spoke to her, his tone softening, although he kept his eyes on her grandmother, holding her furious gaze without flinching. "Is that true?"

She was interested, fairly eaten up with questions about why he'd come and what he wanted to know, if he was angry, and whether he knew how foolish coming here was. But to speak was to defy her grandmother, to belittle her in front of Peter, in front of Monroe. Davinia would be hurt and angry all over again...but oh, Thea did want to hear what Peter had come to say. She did.

"You see?" Davinia spoke first, taking the silence for granted. "You have all you will ever have from Thea. Now, please, do not embarrass her any further by making a scene."

Peter's jaw flexed and Thea knew she had to say something, had to stand up now and be heard.

"Mrs. Carey," Peter said before she could utter a sound. "I believe Thea can speak for herself and I believe she has something to say...if you will only allow her the courtesy of time in which to say it."

Thea looked from one to the other, amazed that Peter would stand up to her grandmother, uncertain as to why he would do such a thing, thrilled to her marrow that he had.

Davinia was also amazed. It showed on her thin, patrician face. But she was neither uncertain nor thrilled. "No one," she said in a voice quivering with outrage. "*No one* speaks to me that way. Monroe, dial the police and inform them that Grace Place has an intruder.'' She turned to sweep from the room, dismissing him in a cutting glance. ''Come, Thea.''

But Thea didn't budge, couldn't have moved if she'd wanted to. Especially not when Peter stopped her grandmother's dramatic exit with a voice as cold as ice. ''Mrs. Carey,'' he said, demanding in just those words that she stop.

And to Thea's astonishment, she did. Turning back, Davinia looked past him, as if it would be beneath her dignity to acknowledge him further.

''Mrs. Carey,'' he repeated. ''I came to talk to Thea and I will not be forced to leave like some riffraff who doesn't deserve a hearing. I allowed you to treat me that way the other night. I won't allow it again.''

''Young man,'' Davinia said coldly, her gaze sweeping him with haughty disdain. ''You *are* riffraff and you have nothing to say about what is and isn't allowed in this house. Now, either you leave or I will have you forceably removed.''

''If I leave, Mrs. Carey, I'm taking Thea with me.''

Thea had been looking from one to the other, but now her eyes fastened on Peter, held on to him as if he were a lifeline, the only thing between her and a drowning oblivion. ''You are?'' she whispered, amazed at this astounding possibility.

His gaze came to her again, tender and caring and wonderfully steady. ''I am,'' he said.

''What *right* do you have to come into my home and make such a startling assumption?'' Davinia demanded. "As if my granddaughter would consent to accompany you anywhere against my wishes."

Peter continued to look at Thea, a faint smile on his handsome mouth. "Do you want to go with me, Thea?"

Her knees were quivering. Her whole body was trembling. With fear. With excitement. With dread. With anticipation. With...hope.

"Can't you see you are scaring the child half to death?"

"She is not a child, Mrs. Carey. Thea is a woman fully capable of making her own decisions."

"Thea, I want you to go to your room. Now."

Thea couldn't move, couldn't stop staring into Peter Braddock's green eyes, into his so handsome face, into the extraordinary reality that he wasn't backing down. "Thea," he said again, even more gently than before. "Do you want to go with me?"

She managed the barest of nods, a mere inclination of movement. *Yes,* she thought. *Yes,* she willed herself to say.

"Don't even consider it, Theadosia." Davinia's tone carried the heavy implications of a threat. "I want you to go to your room. This young man is angry with me because I know who he is and who he pretends to be."

"And who am I, Mrs. Carey?" The thread of steely pride wound through Peter's voice, erecting a barrier of dignity around him, cautioning her to take care.

"Archer Braddock's grandson? James Braddock's son?"

"You, young man, are the product of an adulterous affair and therefore, unworthy of the name you claim as your own."

Peter inhaled sharply and Thea turned to look at her grandmother, unable to believe she had uttered such an ugly, vindictive statement. The trembling turned inward, made Thea's stomach clench and her mouth go dry. "Grandmother," she whispered so softly no one seemed to hear. Or maybe they wouldn't have heard had she shouted.

"Unworthy, perhaps," Peter answered in a voice of deadly calm. "But a Braddock, nevertheless, and...the man who intends to marry your granddaughter."

This time Davinia was the one to catch her breath.

Thea was unable to breathe at all. She thought, in fact, she might never breathe again.

But Davinia recovered quickly, apoplectic with this new outrage. "If you believe I'll consent to such a preposterous match, you aren't nearly as smart as you obviously think you are. My granddaughter deserves a better man than you could ever hope to be."

"I agree with you, Mrs. Carey. But I mean to ask her to marry me, anyway."

"Over my dead body."

Peter inclined his head, his eyes as icy with anger as Davinia's. "I hope it won't come to that," he said.

"But no matter what threats you make, either now or later, this decision belongs to Thea."

She was so still she thought they might not even remember she was there. She wasn't even sure she wanted them to remember. But then Peter turned to her, his eyes clear with purpose. "Thea? Do you want to marry me?"

And before she could stop it, her voice found its way out, rang solidly, clearly, before anyone else could speak for her. "Yes," she said. "Yes."

Chapter Six

"You'll never believe what I just heard!"

Ilsa looked up from her desk as Ainsley came into the office, blond curls fairly bouncing with excitement, the secret, like effervescence, bubbling up and out of her.

"Peter Braddock is going to marry Thea Berenson," Ilsa said, circumventing any thought her apprentice might have of making this a guessing game. "This coming Saturday."

"I knew you'd know the whole story." Ainsley dropped into the chair in front of Ilsa's desk, blue eyes dancing with curiosity and the possibility Ilsa would tell *all*. "I do wish you would have told me, though, so I didn't have to hear it from Miranda, but what happened? Miranda said *she* heard they got caught in Thea's bedroom by none other than old Mrs. Carey, herself, and that now Peter's being strong-armed into marrying her. But I told Miranda that didn't sound like anything Peter would do. Or Thea, either, for that matter. But that's the story going around and so..." She leaned forward in high-energy anticipation, "is *any* of it true?"

Ilsa was sick at heart over the whole episode. Sorry she'd ever even thought about the *possibility* of Peter and Thea, sorry she'd mentioned it to Archer, sorry she hadn't been able to think of any way to stop Peter from facing off against Davinia. "Ainsley," she said now, because she wanted her assistant to understand. "Not every *introduction of possibilities* has a happy ending. I was wrong to let this one go forward against my own very strong reservations."

"But I had the same idea about Peter and Thea." Ainsley scooted forward in the chair, all eagerness and empathy. "I did. Remember at Angela's wedding? I asked you if it was all right if I did a little behind the scenes matchmaking? I was talking about Thea! I was! Honest. And I thought if I could help her some, you know, with makeup and clothes and stuff, that maybe Peter would think of her in a new way. Really, I did. I thought of that exact same possibility. And our intuition must have been right on some level at least or they wouldn't be getting married."

Enthusiasm was a good thing, Ilsa reminded herself. She'd brought Ainsley into IF Enterprises for that very reason. The business needed new ideas, new angles, new possibilities, an infusion of spunk. But this thing with Peter and Thea...well, it wouldn't work. This wasn't a love match. It wasn't even a marriage of convenience. Not for Peter, not for Thea, not for their families. It was Peter showing Davinia she couldn't humiliate him and get away with it. Period.

James agreed on that point.

Archer agreed on that point.

Bryce, in person, and Adam, by long distance, agreed the marriage was a bad idea.

But Peter would hear none of their arguments against it. He'd proposed and been accepted. Congratulations was all that was left to be said.

Ilsa looked across the table at Ainsley's bright-eyed eagerness to believe in yet another fairy tale and managed a rueful smile. "Thea is staying with me until Saturday," she said. "If you could go over sometime this afternoon and persuade her to choose something to wear to the wedding, that would be a big help."

"I can do that." Ainsley beamed with excitement as she bounced up from the chair. "I'd *love* to do that."

"I hope you can convince her to go shopping because…" Ilsa let the sentence trail away as she glanced past her apprentice and caught sight of James in the doorway.

"Hello, Ilsa," he said. "May I come in?"

"Of course." She rose, standing behind the solid safety of her desk, trying to be professional even if she suddenly felt like a tongue-tied schoolgirl. "James, you remember Ainsley Danville, my new assistant?"

"Yes, of course, I do." James's smile brightened the whole room, perhaps even the whole world. "I used to be very good friends with your dad. We were in school together years and years ago and concocted quite a few ill-advised shenanigans between us. There was one particular week, I believe, when we spent more time in the headmaster's office than in the classroom.''

Ainsley dimpled with delight. ''You don't know how happy I am to hear that, Mr. Braddock, because the way my father tells it, he was a model student.''

''He certainly became a model philanthropist,'' James said diplomatically. ''The last I heard he and your mother were in Sarajevo.''

''They're in Ethiopia now, but this year they've promised to be at home with us for the holidays. Maybe you and Dad could get together and talk about old times.''

''I'd like that.''

''Ainsley?'' Ilsa asked. ''Would you excuse us please?''

''Oh, right, Mrs. Fairchild. I'll just go on with that…uh, project…we were discussing, shall I?''

''I'd appreciate anything you can do,'' she said and Ainsley was off and running, closing the office door behind her, before Ilsa changed her mind. Not that Ilsa would. There was nothing to lose by letting Ainsley turn her enthusiasm on Peter's chosen bride. At best, she might be able to bring Thea out of the doldrums she'd been in ever since her arrival in East Side. And at worst…well, the situation could hardly *get* worse no matter what Ainsley or anyone else did. ''Would you like something to drink, James? Coffee, perhaps?''

''Thank you, no.'' He stood, hovering almost, although there was nothing hesitant in his set and solemn expression. "May I sit?"

She nodded and he took the chair Ainsley had just vacated. Suddenly, the room, a normally spacious, comfortable place, seemed to shrink all around Ilsa and the air fairly jumped to attention. Something had changed between one breath and the next.

Or maybe it was simply the thudding rhythm of her own heartbeat.

Which was silly, since she was seldom fooled by attraction in any of its many disguises. There was no denying her heart had always had a foolish spot for this man, but her head had always known better. She eased down into her own chair, clasped her hands on top of the desk, looked at him and wondered how old a woman had to get before she gained some degree of immunity to the Braddock charm. "I imagine," she said, "you've come to talk to me about Peter and Thea."

His smile held all the nuance of a shrug. "I've come," he said, "to ask you to convince Thea not to marry my son."

Ilsa sighed, wishing anything in life could be so simple. "A monumental task, especially as Thea seems to be in a blind stupor and hasn't said ten words in the three days and nights she's been at my house."

"What does she say?"

"'I'm sorry,' and 'thank you.' Sometimes a combination of the two."

"No word from Davinia?"

"Unless you count a notification from her attorney, advising Thea she'll lose her inheritance if she marries Peter."

James shook his head. "Crazy old woman."

"Poor Thea."

"Not if she marries Peter." James pursed his lips, allowing trouble to etch its line across his brow. "But this can't be a happy arrangement for her, either. Please do whatever you can to persuade her, Ilsa."

"And if I can't?"

"Then I'll put on my best tux, a glad face and wish Peter all the luck in the world. I'm hardly the one to be critical of his choice, regardless of the circumstances."

She loved that James freely admitted he hadn't set the best example for his sons and yet, still somehow managed to convey his absolute and unwavering love for them each and every time he spoke their names.

"I'll talk to her," Ilsa agreed. "Although you probably shouldn't count on that having much effect."

"What about if I count on dinner...with you?"

The air changed again, became thicker with an expectation Ilsa recognized and did not want to name. "Is that a threat? I persuade Thea or else..."

His smile coaxed her good humor. "I was hoping you'd view it more as a long overdue invitation, but if a threat gets you to agree to go out with me..." His shrug was as charming as the slightest hint of uncertainty in his eyes.

"Are you asking me on a date, James?"

"High time, don't you think?"

She bit her tongue to keep from saying, *"Yes, yes, of course, I'll go,"* and asked instead, "Did Archer suggest it?"

His surprise was too real to be feigned. "Dad? No, as a matter of fact, I thought of it all on my own. I'll even confess there was a time I thought you and my dad were...well, let's put it nicely and say...a *couple.*"

She laughed. "Archer and *me?* You, of all people, James, should know there's never been room in his life for any woman except your mother. It's funny the idea would ever even cross your mind."

"Yes, well, we Braddock men sometimes get strange ideas about women. And while I realize I've been the standard bearer in that department in the past, at the moment, Peter is the prime example." James's smile faltered, then returned in full measure. "Since you didn't say an emphatic, no, I'll take that as a good sign. For dinner."

She decided to lay her doubts on the table. "As a professional matchmaker who deals in possibilities, I have to advise you the odds aren't good on anything developing other than the friendship we already enjoy."

He got to his feet, a tall, distinguished man who'd weathered joy and sorrow, good choices and bad, and who still made her heart beat a little faster than it ought. "I've been a fool for lesser things, Ilsa. I think I'll take my chances."

Once again, she couldn't breathe. Or think.

But fortunately, he continued. "In the meantime, while you're considering the *possibilities* for us, see what you can do with Thea."

"I will," she said, hardly above a whisper, and with a nod and a smile, he walked away, leaving her to wonder exactly what she'd just agreed to.

THEA DIDN'T LIKE TO SHOP.

She didn't know how, for one thing, because she'd never had the opportunity to learn, nor anyone to teach her. She'd worn uniforms all through school and at home, her grandmother believed in the adage of "waste not, want not," which meant as long as there were clothes in the closets at Grace Place, there was no reason to shop for more. Thea's mother had apparently been a very good shopper because there was plenty of expensive, made-to-last-a-lifetime clothes in the closets, even if the newest of them was still a quarter of a century out of date. Any purchase Thea had ever made on her own, out of the small allowance she received monthly, had been subject to Davinia's critical eye, and even if it was eventually deemed suitable for a lady, Thea could never wear it with any degree of pleasure once she'd been made aware of its flaws.

And that was the other reason Thea didn't shop. Nothing looked the way she imagined it would. She wasn't tall or elegant or graceful. She wasn't petite or cute or pretty. She was so ordinary in appearance, in fact, even the best fabrics and the most classic of designs hung on her with a lackluster indifference. It was

easier just to wear her mother's old clothes and pretend
she didn't mind, than to pine for a stylish look she
could never hope to achieve.

And now, by the flicker of dismay in Ainsley's
bright blue eyes, Thea could tell that the wedding gown
she'd just put on was no improvement over the last one
or the one before that. But she turned to the mirror,
anyway, hoping that just once she'd see someone other
than her own mediocre self.

"Hmm," Ainsley murmured diplomatically as she
eyed the dress.

"Maybe something less...fluffy," the bridal shop
clerk suggested.

Thea wanted to suggest they just forget about bridal
gowns and all go out for an ice cream, but she didn't.
She just stood there, letting them fuss and figure and
evaluate each gown in turn. She knew no dress was
going to look right, because *she* wasn't right. That was
simply all there was to it. Maybe if the situation had
been different, maybe if she was really and truly a
bride, then it might have mattered. She might have
cared one way or the other. But none of this was real.
It was a long extended daydream, a rather lovely daydream, at that. But still, she knew Peter didn't want to
marry her and she knew he'd call a halt to all this
craziness long before Saturday.

Never mind that Saturday was only two days away.
Never mind that she'd burned a bridge just in pretending she believed the wedding would actually take
place. Her grandmother might never speak to her again,

might never even let her in the door of Grace Place again, might never ever forgive her. Thea had been thinking a lot about that ever since Peter had taken her to Mrs. Fairchild's and left her there with his repeated assurances that *"everything will be all right."* She wasn't certain she believed him, but it was nice to hear just the same.

He'd been in Boston all week, staying at his apartment there, working in his office at Braddock Architectural Designs. Thea knew that only because he'd mentioned it every time he called to talk to her, which had been surprisingly frequent...twice, sometimes even three times a day. There was no doubt Peter believed she was happy to be away from gloomy old Grace Place and her gloomy old grandmother. And maybe she was. But she really missed her cats.

"What about something not so...white?" Ainsley asked the clerk, who pursed her lips, obviously straining to think of any dress in the inventory that might look tolerably bridal on Thea.

"There is one," the clerk said hesitantly. "It's very plain and an odd sort of color for a wedding dress. It would be a lovely gown for someone with your blond hair and fair skin, Ms. Danville, and I don't know, but it might be all right for your friend. It does happen to be in her size. If there were time for alterations to be made, of course, I'm sure we could find something more suitable, but..."

"But there isn't time," Ainsley confirmed with a smile despite the slightest edge of impatience in her voice. "So let's try the gown you mentioned, shall we? Is that all right with you, Thea?"

Thea was used to being talked about as if she wasn't there. It happened to her all the time, and she appreciated Ainsley's attempt to include her in this conversation even if the clerk had long since dismissed her as irrelevant. But she truly didn't care if they left this store with a dress or not, except she wouldn't for the world want to hurt Ainsley's feelings. "Let's just take that one," Thea suggested, determined not to see herself in yet another awful dress. "I'm sure it will be fine for what I need."

"But…" Ainsley began and then, catching Thea's eye in the mirror, she nodded. "Yes," she said. "Let's take it, sight unseen, and if we don't like it we'll bring it back tomorrow. Steam and press it," she told the clerk. "Mr. Braddock's chauffeur, Benson, will pick it up later this afternoon."

"Braddock?" The clerk couldn't disguise her recognition of the name nor her surprise as her gaze turned, unbelievingly, to Thea.

"Braddock," Ainsley repeated, her dimple flashing Thea's way with a touch of satisfaction. "As in Braddock Industries, Braddock Hall… Shall we write that down for you?"

"No, I'll take care of everything," the woman said, suddenly eager to please. "Is there anything else, Ms. Berenson? A veil, perhaps? Undergarments? Some intimate apparel for the wedding night?"

Thea's heart suddenly whisked into a frenzied

rhythm. *Wedding night?* She hadn't thought about that, hadn't thought about so many things, hadn't a clue what would happen to her after Peter called off the wedding.

"Ms. Berenson?" The clerk offered a solicitous hand to help her off the dais.

But Thea shook her head mutely, and stepped down by herself, stumbling a little over the unaccustomed pouf of the bridal gown. She waved away any assistance from the clerk or Ainsley, and scurried into the dressing room, eager to get out of the dress and out of the store. What had she been thinking to come on this shopping trip, anyway?

She didn't like shopping.

So why was she here, shopping for a wedding gown to wear at a wedding that wasn't ever, no matter how hard she dreamed, going to be real?

"As a HIDEOUT, this place leaves a lot to be desired."

Peter turned from the window of his office to see his oldest brother in the doorway. "Adam," he said with genuine pleasure. "What are you doing here in Boston?"

Adam's smile was relaxed, easy, light years removed from the Type A tension that had marked his every expression just six months ago. But that had been Adam BK, as Bryce liked to call it. *Adam, before Katie.* A clear delineation. Peter thought his brother looked good. Better than good. Happy…all the way through his heart and out the other side. "Now, Peter, you didn't think Katie and I would let you get married without us, do you?"

Married. Peter's stomach clenched at the word, but he didn't let it show as he moved forward to shake his brother's hand and give him a quick, affectionate, welcome-home hug. "I'm glad you're here," he said. "How long are you and Katie going to stay this time?"

"Indefinitely, as it turns out." Adam's smile broadened, his face flushed a little with excitement. "Katie's pregnant."

"Congratulations." Peter cuffed Adam on the shoulder. "That's great news. So does that mean the extended honeymoon is over?"

"With Katie, life is always going to be one long extended honeymoon. The baby's an early bonus, believe me."

Peter envied Adam his confidence in love, just as he'd always envied him his confidence in life. "But you're going to stay at the Hall at least until the baby comes?"

"Katie has a couple more places on her list of things to see before that happens, but by early spring, I think we'll be back for good. My wife has a new appreciation for tradition, it seems, and she really wants the baby to grow up at Braddock Hall. Of course, Grandfather thinks that's a grand idea. He's encouraging her to pursue this scheme she has of opening a tea room and gift shop in downtown Sea Change."

"What about you, Adam? Don't tell me you'd be content to watch the baby while your wife works. You can't have changed that much.'' Peter grinned. ''I know for a fact the people of Sea Change would be happy for you to take Bryce's place on the town council. He aggravates them all just for the fun of it.''

''I know. Dad was telling me about the brick project and the fiasco that's turned into. And to be honest, Peter, Bryce has already talked to me about the possibility of stepping down as CEO, too, anytime I'm ready to take over.''

''I can't say I'm surprised. Our brother has never made any secret of the fact he prefers limiting his responsibilities so he has plenty of time for other things. And now that he's married and has Cal, I think he's feeling the pinch of too many time constraints.''

Adam nodded agreement. ''That's the idea I got from him, too. I'll be the first to admit I'm beginning to miss the challenge of working, even though I'll never be so totally consumed by that high-powered lifestyle again, not with Katie to keep me sane. But I don't want Bryce to feel like I'm eager to shove him aside, either. He's done a great job, certainly better than I thought he could.''

''He has. Maybe we ought to think about combining our philanthropic trusts under the umbrella of a single foundation and putting Bryce in charge of it. He'd be great at that, lots of PR for him to do and not so much pressurized responsibility.''

''Good idea,'' Adam said. ''We should talk it over with Grandfather and Dad. See what they think.''

"Maybe this weekend," Peter suggested. "Since we'll all be home."

"Except you'll be sort of busy, what with getting married and all."

"Oh. Right." And there it was. The reason Adam was here now. Peter didn't have a doubt that his oldest brother had been designated official spokesman by the other Braddock men. He was here to point out the flaw in Peter's thinking, the mistake he was about to make if he married Thea. They'd all had a run at him in one way or another this past week. It was Adam's turn, and Peter decided he might as well get this over with and remove the last *if* from their thinking. "Can you believe all three of us getting married in the same year? Only months apart? Pretty amazing when you think what confirmed bachelors we all were a year ago."

"Amazing, indeed." Adam frowned. "And in your case, a bit mystifying as well."

"Not really. You wanted to marry Katie. Bryce wanted to marry Lara. I want to marry Thea. Pretty simple."

"Oh, come on, Peter. You don't want to marry Thea."

"That's where you're wrong, Adam."

"You're not in love with her. You hardly know her."

"I know this is right, Adam. I can't…I won't…offer any other explanation. Not to you, not to Grandfather, not to Dad. Not to anyone."

"Be her champion then, if you must, but don't marry

her. That's the wrong solution to her problem and the start of a whole new set of problems for you. Believe me.''

"I happen to believe it's the only solution to her problem and the answer to a question I've been asking myself for years. I'm marrying Thea on Saturday, Adam, and that's the end of this conversation.''

Adam eyed Peter, his doubts written clearly across his brow. "All right, if that's what you want, I'll say congratulations and wish you luck. But Peter, please reconsider. You don't have to do this.''

"I do," he said firmly because it was true. "So tell me about the places on Katie's list, the ones you still have to visit?''

Adam relinquished his mission with good grace, as a gentleman should. "Next up," he said, "is Nome. Don't ask me why she wants to see Alaska at this time of year, and I'm trying to persuade her to postpone the trip, but you know Katie. She's determined to…''

As the tension eased under the tales of Adam's and Katie's big adventure, Peter figured he'd weathered the last of his family's overt objections. They would say nothing else to him about it.

Now all that was left was to get through the wedding without Davinia showing up and making a scene…although technically, that was something a lady would never do. But Peter wouldn't put it past her.

THEA WAS STILL waiting for the knock on the door when she heard the music begin downstairs.

"That's our cue." Ainsley, looking cute as a rose-bud in a bright pink Escada suit, picked up the bridal bouquet and held it out to Thea with a smile. "Are you sure you don't want to take a look in the mirror? Really, Thea, that dress is perfect."

Thea shook her head. No, she didn't want to look at herself and see what everyone else was too nice to say. They'd all been so nice to her. Ainsley, Mrs. Fairchild, all of the Braddocks...Archer, James, Adam, Katie, Lara, Bryce and Peter. Most of all, Peter. But she'd thought he would come to her before now, explain how he couldn't marry her, had never really intended to marry her, knew she'd understand why marriage wasn't the answer.

And she would have understood. Truly.

"Ready, Thea?" Ainsley was opening the door of the upstairs bedroom, stepping out, walking with a measured beat to the top of the staircase...starting down.

Thea didn't know what to do except follow.

Her knees quivered with every step and she had to walk slowly because the dress was long and swished in swirls of delicious silk about her feet. Ainsley had insisted she wear these dainty little shoes that were half ballet slipper, half house-shoe and Thea was overly conscious of their tendency to slip on the marble tiles. Ainsley had done something to her hair, too, pinned it up somehow, stuck little twigs of baby's breath in it and now the topknot felt heavy and as if it was about to tumble down in her face at any minute. She'd managed to keep her black-framed glasses, despite Ainsley's subtle suggestion that perhaps, this once, she could get by without them. And she could have...but she was glad now for their familiar weight on her nose. Her breath came in short, shallow puffs as she made the turn and looked down at the great hall below.

She expected Peter to be waiting there at the bottom of the wide stairs, waiting to tell her he couldn't marry her. But it was Archer Braddock who smiled up at her. Archer, who waited to escort her into the library. Thea took a deep breath, trying to think what to do. Ainsley had reached the bottom step and was even now making the turn toward the library. Music from a string quartet floated about like butterflies, drawing Thea down one step and then another.

This wasn't the way she'd thought it would be.

She'd thought Peter would stop it.

Or her grandmother.

But she reached the landing and crossed it, took another step down toward the bottom.

Maybe Peter was waiting until she reached him. Maybe he would make an announcement then that this was all a mistake, a figment of Thea's imagination. But the stairs beneath her slippers were solid, as was Archer's hand reaching out to help her down the last few steps. And when she turned with him, she could see the people inside the library, standing, watching as she slowly approached the doorway, and they were real, too.

Peter was there, ahead. Standing straight and tall in

front of the minister, watching her, his lips curving in a nervous smile, so handsome she couldn't breathe. She'd always thought he had impeccable taste, but in his tuxedo, he looked splendid. Which was another reason this couldn't be real. Peter Braddock should have a wife who was beautiful. Thea wasn't, so this could not be real. He could not be marrying her. Not her.

But then the music stopped and Archer patted her hand. The next thing she knew, Peter had taken her hand in his and she was making the last decisive step, facing the minister, who opened his book and cleared his throat.

"Dearly beloved…"

The bouquet of fresh flowers shook in her fist and a petal broke free and fell, end over end, to the floor. She stared at it, a sliver of palest pink, lying there, out of place on the richly colored pile of the oriental rug. It didn't belong in this warm inviting room any more than she did.

And if Peter wasn't going to stop this, if he meant—unbelievably—to marry her, then it was up to her to save him from whatever madness had claimed him.

But how to do it without making a scene? A lady never caused a scene. Ever. So could she manage a laugh and say, *"All right, no one here really believed we were going through with this, did they?"* Did she run from the room like a coward? Break out in wild sobbing? Faint dead away?

That last, at least, seemed like a viable option. Her

breath was coming still in short, shallow gasps and if she stood here much longer, she really might faint.

"Theadosia Elsinora Grace Berenson," the minister intoned solemnly. "Will you take this man to be your lawfully married husband?"

Time was up. Thea looked up at Peter, gathered courage she didn't know she had, and said what had to be said. "No. I'm sorry, Peter. But I can't do this."

And then she fainted.

Chapter Seven

"Thea? Wake up, Thea." Peter's voice pulled her out of a warm oblivion with soft insistence. "Come on, Thea, wake up."

She blinked and opened her eyes to see him leaning over her, cupping her head in the palm of one hand, looking at her with a glint of near panic in his startlingly green eyes. "What happened?" she whispered.

"You said you couldn't marry me and then you fainted."

"Oh." She closed her eyes for a moment, remembering, then blinked them open again. "Where are we?"

"In my bedroom."

She was on the bed, she realized, with him sitting beside her—leaning, really—his hips wedged against hers, his arm supporting her shoulders, his hand under her head, tenderness in every nuance of his touch. "Did...did everyone leave?"

"Leave? No, they're waiting downstairs. As soon as

you feel up to it, we'll go back down and continue with the wedding.''

The wedding. She bit her lip and reached up to push her glasses farther up her nose. But the glasses weren't there. The only protection she had from the gentle concern in his eyes, and she'd lost them. ''My...my glasses?''

''On the bedside table,'' he said. ''I took them off for you.''

''Oh.'' She didn't know whether to thank him or ask him to give them back.

''Are you all right? I can call a doctor if you don't feel well.''

''No.'' She shook her head...and felt the sensual response of his fingers moving against her hair. ''I'm fine,'' she said hoping he'd take his hand from beneath her head and, at the same time, hoping he would keep it there always. ''Just...just nervous.''

His smile fell over her like sunlight, warming her through. ''Me, too. But I think that's pretty normal under the circumstances.''

He was surely the most handsome of bridegrooms ever, but she couldn't let him do this. Not for her. ''One of those circumstances being that you can't want to marry me.''

''Thea,'' he murmured, stopping her heartbeat with his tenderness. He lowered her head to the pillow and pulled his hand free, placed it flat on the bed beside her. ''Look, I realize this is probably not the way you pictured your wedding day, but I do want to marry you.

Your grandmother is suffocating you and you have to get out from under her thumb before your spirit gives up and dies and you're trapped for the rest of your life. I can help you. I want to do this. Honestly, I do. It feels right to me and believe me, I've spent my entire life looking for something, *anything*, that feels this right. Please trust me when I tell you there's nothing I want more than to marry you. Now. Today.''

Hardly the tender words of love and sweet pledges of forever a bride wanted to hear on her wedding day, but for someone like Thea, who'd never expected any man would want to marry her, much less someone as perfect as Peter Braddock, they were the most romantic words she'd ever heard. She loved the nobility of his gesture, the sincerity in his voice, the earnestness of his expression, the intensity of his belief—mistaken as it undoubtedly was—but most of all she loved him for thinking she was worth such a sacrifice.

"Peter," she said. "Please don't think I'm unappreciative, but I can't let you do this.''

"Yes, you can, Thea. Take a deep breath and repeat what you said the first time I asked you to marry me. Yes. You said...yes.''

The difference then, of course, was that he'd said, *do you want to marry me?* And it would have been a lie to say no. The rest had happened so quickly after that—her grandmother banishing her from Grace Place, leaving with Peter, letting him take her to Mrs. Fairchild's house, permitting Ainsley to persuade her to shop for a wedding dress, allowing time and then more time to go by without saying the *"no"* that needed to be said. "You can't want this, Peter. It...it wouldn't be a...a real marriage."

"It will be whatever you want it to be, Thea. That's the thing, see...it's your chance to be whatever you want with no one to remind you of what *they* want. Or how you should act, or how you should feel, or what you should do, or not do, or think, or not think. You don't have to commit your life to me. You don't have to do one damn thing to please me or anyone else. You don't have to be scared anymore. You can choose the life you want to have. Please, I want to give you this, Thea. It's important to me to do that. I know this may be hard for you to understand right now, but this is my chance, too. I once was powerless to help someone I loved, but it's within my power to help you. And I want to do that, Thea. Let me help you help yourself."

No one had ever asked what she wanted. Or if she wanted a life different from the one she had. And it was tempting—so tempting—to accept his offer and not think about the fact that tomorrow or the next day or the day after that, he would wonder why he'd taken on her problems, why he'd saddled himself with her as his wife.

His wife.

Even the words held music...like the soaring notes of an aria that were at once both painful and satisfying. It would be so easy to say yes, to let him save her and reject the responsibility of saving herself. "Peter, I

can't…'' she began only to stop when something
landed on the bed with a muffled, *thump*.

"I was afraid of that," Peter said, smiling. "I was
saving this for a surprise after the wedding, but looks
like Ally has other ideas. As usual." He scooped the
calico up in his hand and set her down on Thea's chest,
where the kitten immediately moved up to press her
moist pink nose against Thea's chin. She licked Thea
with a rough tongue and then purred like a buzz saw.

"Ally," Thea said, stroking the soft, spotted fur, her
gaze seeking Peter's with teary pleasure. "You rescued
Ally for me."

He looked a trifle embarrassed. "I rescued the whole
family of cats, but before you start thanking me pro-
fusely for risking life and limb to do it, I'll admit I had
inside help."

"Monroe," she said, comforted by the thought. "He
and Sadie smuggled them out to you."

"Something like that." He stroked Ally, too, and she
turned, equal-opportunity cat that she was, to curl herself around his hand and purr even louder. "The others
are still a little cautious in their new surroundings, so
I imagine they're going to remain under the bed for a
while."

"Thank you, Peter." She blinked back tears, not
wanting him to see how much this meant to her.

"My pleasure," he said…and she could see that it
was true. It pleased him to have done this for her and
she knew in that moment, she would love him forever.

"Peter," she started only to be interrupted again by a ruckus on the other side of the door.

"Do not patronize me, sir. I will see my granddaughter whether you *announce* me or not!"

The door opened and Abbott, looking flushed and furious, said crisply. "I'm sorry, Mr. Peter, but Mrs. Carey wishes to see—"

"Thea!" Davinia pushed past the butler and stepped into the room. "What has happened to you?"

Guilt flooded Thea with immediate and familiar intensity as she struggled to sit up. Peter rose from the bed as the door opened and he reached down now to help her gain her feet. "Mrs. Carey," he said. "I'm glad you could make it to the wedding. Thea had a little fainting spell, but she seems to be fine, now."

"Are you married?" Davinia asked sharply, her clear gaze steady on Thea. "Or did you come to your senses before it was too late?"

"No." Thea pushed the word past the knot in her throat.

"Well, which is it?" Davinia snapped. "Did you marry him or not?"

"Not yet." Peter braced Thea with an arm about her waist and a steady grip on her clasped and trembling hands. "We were about to go downstairs when you… knocked."

Davinia said nothing, but her gaze narrowed as Ally stretched herself and jumped off the bed to twine luxuriously around Peter's pant leg. "What is that cat doing here? I told Monroe to dispose of it and the others.''

''Yes, well, Monroe and I had a better idea.'' Peter squeezed Thea's hand, either as comfort or warning, she couldn't tell which. Her grandmother had been going to get rid of her cats. Thea could hardly believe Davinia would be so cruel.

''Thea and I are pleased you accepted the invitation to be at our wedding,'' Peter continued. ''If you'll kindly go with Abbott, he will show you the way to the library, where in just a few minutes, Thea and I will say our vows. We've saved you a seat beside Grandfather…and I'm sure you know how distressing it is for him when any guest at Braddock Hall is late.''

Davinia ignored him. ''Thea, if you come home to Grace Place with me now, you may bring those…animals with you. Come along, now. Monroe is waiting for us in the car.''

Thea stared at her grandmother, knowing the choices before her were both wrong. How could she go back? How could she stay?

''What do *you* want, Thea?'' Peter asked softly.

She turned her head to look at him and in doing so, caught a glimpse of herself in the mirror. But that couldn't be her. She closed her eyes and opened them again, but the image didn't change. It stayed the same, reflecting a woman in a dress of pearly pink silk that draped her body as if she'd been born to wear it. A dress that gave shape to the slight curves she'd always thought of as boyish and revealed the slope of a neck not nearly as long as she'd always imagined it to be and more graceful in appearance than she would have thought possible. And her hair wasn't falling down, wasn't even very disheveled from her recent lie-down on the bed. Her eyes looked big and brown, framed as they were by mascaraed lashes instead of the old black glasses. Thea inhaled…and was fascinated by the way her breasts lifted beneath the folds of silk that dipped from her shoulders to show just a hint of cleavage. *Cleavage.* She had cleavage.

"Thea," Davinia said. "I'm waiting for you. Come along, now, and put all this nonsense aside."

"No," Thea said, knowing in an instant what she wanted…and what she wanted was to be the woman she saw in the mirror. Not beautiful, or even pretty, but almost…confident. A woman with *possibilities.* "I'm not going with you, Grandmother. I'm going to…" She stopped, turning to Peter, wanting him to understand. But his eyes suddenly lit with relief and…gratitude. She knew then she was going to marry him, after all.

Not because she needed him to save her, but because he needed to save her in order to save himself.

"I'm going to marry Peter," she said, and was surprised at the ring of confidence in her voice. "I hope you'll stay for the wedding, Grandmother, but whether you do or not will make no difference. Isn't that…that right, Peter?"

"Yes," he said, smiling down at her with a touch of surprise and—was it possible—admiration in his eyes. "That's right." He squeezed her hand. "Abbott," he said without taking his gaze from her face. "Would you let Grandfather know Thea and I will be down in a minute?"

"Yes, sir," Abbott said, professional and properly polite as he addressed Davinia. "Mrs. Carey, will you come with me, please?"

Davinia narrowed her gaze on Peter. "You're not good enough for her," she said accusingly. "She deserves more than this...this insult of a marriage."

"She *deserves* to choose and you just heard her say she chooses me."

With a low *humph!* Davinia turned and walked out, her back ramrod straight, defiant even in defeat and self-destructively proud.

Thea's knees quivered from the strain of the last few minutes, but she commanded them to bear up without complaint...and surprisingly, the quivering stopped. She raised her chin, afraid Peter would question her decision or compliment her courage or ask her something she could not answer.

"Your glasses," was all he said, though, indicating she should get them from the bedside table.

"I don't need them, anymore," she said.

Which was, in fact, the truth.

"YOU MAY KISS your bride," the minister concluded.

During the past surreal week, Peter had thought more about this moment than almost any other. What he would do. If he should kiss her. How he should kiss her. A chaste touch to the lips? A more fraternal peck on the cheek? Would one or the other embarrass her? Or give her the wrong idea? He'd pretty much decided a friendly, noncommital hug would be best. But now the moment was here and he knew it had to be a kiss. A real one. In front of all these witnesses, she deserved at least that consideration.

So he put his hands on her shoulders, drew her toward him, and bent to kiss the lips that parted in startled surprise and then…amazingly, softened to sweet acceptance beneath his. Peter had kissed a lot of women, more really than his fair share. But not one of them, ever, had kissed him back with such complete trust, such simple faith. No other woman had curved her body, all willowy and slender and supple, against his, with her only desire being to rely upon his strength and integrity. Thea's kiss awakened a whole world of protective feelings in him and elicited from his body a response he hadn't expected. He wanted the kiss to go on, wanted to explore this new and satisfying sensation, but people were watching and Thea had to be as aware as he was of her grandmother's disapproving glare. Drawing back, he kept his hands supportively on her shoulders and offered her a slightly bemused smile, which she returned with a tremulous and uncertain sigh.

"Hello, Mrs. Braddock," he said, and immediately regretted it when the color washed out of her cheeks and her tentative smile faded like yesterday's sunshine. "It's okay, Thea," he whispered. "Everything will be okay." Then he kissed her again…a chaste, reassuring brush of his lips against hers, which only brought another fleeting wish that there was time for more.

But Calvin, having sat as still as possible for as long as possible, yelled out, "Quit kissin', Uncle Peter, and let's eat cake!"

Which made everyone laugh…except Davinia.

And her granddaughter.

"AH, ILSA, YOU HAVE made me a very happy man." Archer smiled as she settled into the wingback chair next to him and nearest the fire.

"And don't think I'm not well aware of the reason, either." Ilsa leaned across the padded chair arm to whisper conspiratorially. "You saw Davinia Carey eyeing this seat, the same as I did, and you are exceedingly glad that I got here first."

He acknowledged her point with a wry lift of his brows. "I do thank you for that, as well. I've had all of Davinia's dour company I can stomach for one week, although just between us, I think she's behaved better this afternoon than anyone expected."

"How can you say so, Archer? She's hardly said a word that could be considered cordial and she's kept poor Thea on pins and needles just by being here. I don't know why she came in the first place and I certainly don't understand why she's stayed so long."

Archer considered Davinia as she sat stiffly and alone across the room, and he found it in his heart to feel sorry for her. "I imagine she hates to go home to an empty house."

"And who's to blame for that?" Ilsa sighed. "Oh, please, let's not talk about her, anymore. Let's talk about the news that you're going to have a great-grandchild in the spring."

"A second great-grandchild," Archer corrected. "Cal's adoption will be final by then, as well. I owe you more than I could ever repay, Ilsa. Thank you."

"You can credit me all you want with the *introductions of possibilities,* Archer, but I'm not taking any blame for the Braddock baby boom."

Archer chuckled as his gaze found his grandsons, clustered in a casual, comfortable circle with their wives. Adam was laughing at something Peter had said to Bryce and which Katie and Lara seemed to find vastly amusing as well. It was good to see Adam so relaxed, and Archer gave Katie all the credit for her husband's new easygoing demeanor. She had changed him for the better and that was a good thing. As for her, Katie wore the early glow of motherhood with a sweet excitement and Archer loved that she was barefoot now and still went without shoes as often as possible. He was glad Adam hadn't curbed her free spirit or changed her mind about the adventure of living, that he had, in fact, learned to share that adventure with her. Adam couldn't take his eyes off her...or stop smiling. Even when he returned to work—as Archer knew he eventually would—Adam would be a different kind of CEO, a better man at the office and at home.

Bryce responded to Peter's quip and brought laughter to the group all over again. Archer was so proud of

Bryce, so grateful he had found Lara and Cal and recognized them for the missing pieces he needed in his life. Bryce's stint as the man in charge of Braddock Industries had been good for him. He'd always had confidence, but now it seemed a settled thing about him. His playboy days were over and he had nothing else to prove to himself or to anyone and that, too, Archer considered a good thing. Bryce had chosen a beautiful wife, who was more than his match in every way, and yet she looked at him as if he'd hung the moon and every one of the stars. Love should be like that, Archer knew from his own experience…and he was humbled and gratified to see his grandsons experiencing it, too.

And as if that weren't enough, Archer found immense satisfaction in watching Bryce parent Calvin. He'd worried some that Bryce might follow James's example and be an uninvolved father. But that wasn't the case. A four-year-old son seemed to be just what Bryce needed, and he was rising to meet the challenge of fatherhood with an almost unbridled enthusiasm.

Archer's attention turned, finally, to Peter, who looked, if not in love, at least happy. Since the ceremony, he had kept Thea close at his side, already confident in his role as her protector. She was quiet, but not unusually so…and when she looked at Peter, her heart was in her eyes. Archer was frankly amazed Peter didn't seem to notice that his wife was in love with him. But then, this marriage was Peter's journey and he would come to the truth in his own good time. What he'd make of it was anyone's guess. There was no way to know what lay ahead for these newlyweds, but Archer felt in his heart Peter had made the right choice. "You know, Ilsa, had anyone asked me a year ago if even one of my grandsons would be married within the year, I'd have had to say a resounding no. You've made three remarkable matches and I thank you from the bottom of my heart."

"Two remarkable matches," she said. "I'm not proud of this last one."

"You should be. Whatever the outcome of this marriage, Ilsa, it will be a good thing for these two young people. Look at them. I've never seen Peter look so proud or Thea so trusting. Don't doubt yourself, Ilsa. You have a genuine gift when it comes to recognizing the true need of a seeking heart. With Peter, just as with Adam and Bryce, you trusted your intuition. Don't lose faith in it now. I believe we'll all come to consider this match as much a success as the other two."

Her lips curved in a wry smile. "I hope you're right, Archer, because the way this has all come about makes me think I've lost my touch."

"Now that's not what your charming assistant was telling me just a little while ago. Ainsley says you're a genius at matchmaking."

"Ainsley has a lot to learn…most of it having to do with discretion."

He laughed. "She's delightful and tells me she helped Thea pick out her wedding gown."

"She did persuade Thea to go shopping, when I'd

quite given up hope of getting her out of the house at all."

"If Ainsley is responsible for that choice of gown, then you should give her a raise. Thea looks very nice, indeed."

"She does, doesn't she?" Ilsa's voice picked up hope. "Maybe you're right, Archer. Whatever happens between her and Peter, she, at least, is better off now than she was just last week."

"I choose to think Peter is, too, despite all of our worries that he was making a big mistake."

"All right, Dad." James walked up to hand Archer a small snifter of brandy, his evening allotment. "You've monopolized Ilsa long enough. Give the rest of us a chance to talk to her."

"It's not my fault if you're too slow to get her attention." He tilted the glass and watched the brandy swirl, knowing the anticipation of the drink was half of the enjoyment. "We've been discussing Ilsa's success as a matchmaker, James. Perhaps you should consider hiring her to locate a suitable match for you."

"I'll take that under advisement, Dad."

"Your call, of course, James, but Ilsa does have a stellar list of success stories."

"Two of them in this very room. I know, Dad, and I happen to agree with you. Ilsa is...quite amazing."

"*Three* successes," Ilsa said, making it somehow, a challenge...and there was a certain look in her gray eyes, a hint of heightened color in her cheeks, a soft note of flirtation in her voice, *possibilities* in the tilt of her smile.

Archer masked his pleasure by taking a sip of the brandy. Well, well. So he wasn't such a bad match-maker, himself. With a satisfied sigh, he lifted the glass to his lips and sent a thought winging heavenward. *Three down, Janey. One to go.*

"I THOUGHT YOU might like this room." Peter opened the door and flipped the light switch, which turned on both bedside lamps. The bedroom filled with a warm golden glow, looking more inviting by night than it did even during the daytime. "I asked our housekeeper, Ruth, to have it redecorated for you, but I picked out the wallpaper and accessories." He felt uncertain, as if she might not like what he'd chosen, as if the rose and gold patterned drapes and bedding might offend her in some way. "It's not your attic at Grace Place, but maybe it will feel a little like home."

"Thank you," she said, her voice so soft it was barely a whisper.

This was even more awkward than he'd imagined. But he had no idea what he was supposed to say to his *wife* on their wedding night. It had all seemed gallant and romantic until now, a simple solution to all of Thea's problems, but suddenly he was face-to-face with all the things this marriage wasn't going to be. "I thought you'd prefer a little extra privacy, so this suite is about as far from the family section as it gets here at Braddock Hall."

He could have bitten his tongue in two for saying it that way, as if she didn't belong in the south ell with the family, as if he wanted her bedroom as far from his as possible. But she merely nodded and said a faint, "It's very nice, thank you."

"I asked Ruth to put fresh flowers out every day for you." He indicated the vases of fresh flowers from Archer's greenhouse, the artful arrangements of daisies, roses and fragrant orchids. "Grandfather is very proud of his greenhouses. If you ask, I'm sure he'll give you a tour. And if you prefer a certain flower or a...a particular color, all you have to do is ask. I put all the art supplies I could find in Sea Change right there beside the secretary." He indicated the antique writing desk, the basket on the floor next to it. "There're sketch pads and charcoals, pastels and pencils, paints of all kinds, brushes, too. I thought you might want to sketch while you're here. But if you need something else—special brushes or a special kind of canvas or anything—tell Abbott and he'll order it for you." Peter knew he was talking too much, too fast, that he was nervous for reasons he couldn't quite define. Maybe it was the reality of what he—what *they*—had just done. Married. They were married. He was married to Theadosia Berenson. Braddock. Thea Braddock. And she was married to him.

"I thought it would be better not to take a honeymoon trip," he went on as if it was a logical explanation to make on his wedding night. "Everyone pretty well knows the circumstances. In the family, I mean.

Everyone in the family is aware that we…that the wedding…'' He was making a hash of this. And all he'd meant to do was make Thea feel comfortable and easy in her new surroundings. "I have to be in the office this week. There's a project that can't be put off, and I'll be going to Boston every day. I'll come home in the evenings though. Every evening, so don't worry that you'll have to face the family alone.''

She looked at him then, her eyes startlingly big and richly brown without the distraction of the big, black glasses. "I'm not worried, Peter," she said. "I understand.''

He felt even worse, if that were possible. "I really do have to work, Thea. If we could have planned the wedding for later, I could have arranged time off for a honeymoon, but I'm the lead architect on this Boston project and I have to be there to oversee it at this stage.''

"I understand," she repeated, standing just inside the doorway, still in the lustrous pearl of a wedding gown, although it seemed a little rumpled now. The sprigs of white she'd worn in her hair were gone. He didn't know what had happened to them. He'd noticed on previous occasions that when she was nervous—as she apparently often was whenever he was around— she tucked and pulled and fidgeted with her hair, so maybe she'd pulled the baby's breath out a little at a time. Or the sprigs had fallen out on their own. Her hair was coming down from its upswept styling, too, a straggle here and there, the top part slightly askew. She clutched Ally close against her, scratching the calico absently behind the ears. "I never expected a honeymoon trip, Peter. I know this isn't a...a real marriage."

And there, in a nutshell, Thea had summed up all the ways this marriage was wrong. He'd thought he was justified in doing this, still felt in his heart it was the right thing to have done, the only way he could have rescued Thea from her grandmother. But if he'd only taken her from a lonely attic at Grace Place and placed her in a lonely bedroom at Braddock Hall, then what had he really accomplished? She was still an outsider, still a wallflower, blending into the background, not feeling she had a right to claim anyone's attention. Not even her husband's.

"Please, Peter," she said, misunderstanding his sudden stricken silence. "You don't have to look so apologetic. This bedroom is very nice. The cats and I will be happy here, I'm sure."

His mouth went dry with remorse, partly because she thought a bedroom was all she had a right to expect out of this marriage, partly because until this moment, he'd thought so, too. "We should have talked this through," he said. "This is not how I meant for it to be."

"Oh, Peter." She moved to the bed and let Ally down to wander the floral print of the comforter. "I like the wallpaper and the bedding and...and the whole room. Really." Her hand trailed across the comforter, her fingertips investigating the texture of it. "Even if you'd asked me, I'm sure I couldn't have chosen any-thing I'd like more.''

''I'm not talking about the way the room's deco-rated, Thea, although I shouldn't have presumed to make that decision for you, either. I meant, I should have talked to you about getting married and living here and whether you wanted to be...alone.''

Her hand stilled, the fabric bunching slightly beneath the sudden tension in her fingers. ''I...'' Her voice trailed off, but then she raised her head and lifted her chin as she met his gaze. ''Don't feel sorry for me, Peter. And don't offer me something you're not willing to give.''

He knew a grin was totally inappropriate, but couldn't hold his back. To see Thea so resolute, to hear the faint, but definite trace of determination in her voice surprised and pleased him. And what could she possibly ask for that he wouldn't be willing to give? ''If you want me to stay and keep you company, Thea, all you have to do is say so. We can play cards or you can show me how to sketch or we'll teach Ally to chase a ball or do tricks or something. There's no reason for you to be alone tonight if you don't want to be.''

Her eyes narrowed on his face, but he saw the way her hand trembled before she gathered a fistful of comforter into a tight ball within her palm. He saw, too, a hard swallow convulse in her throat, and he was sorry he'd given in to the impulse to smile.

''I don't want to be alone, Peter, but...''

''Fine,'' he said, wanting her to know she could ask

him anything, trust him with her feelings. "I'll stay and we'll—"

"But…" She interrupted his reassurance, made his heart beat a little faster with the sudden fearful fire in her dark eyes. "If you stay, we're not playing cards or playing with the cat or…or anything like that." Her voice quivered and she paused to swallow again. "Peter, I…I want a…a wedding night."

Any hint of a smile faded quickly from his lips and, while his first impulse was to run like hell, it was instantly followed by the realization that wild horses couldn't have dragged him out of there. *A wedding night.* She couldn't have meant… But what else *could* she mean? And did she have any idea what she was asking? How could she know, virginal and innocent as she was? And what was wrong with him that his body's instant reaction had been the yes of desire and not a resounding no? And how was he going to refuse without crushing this first defiant glimmer of self-determination? "Thea," he began, cautious not to sound condescending or overly moralistic. "You can't mean that."

She lowered her gaze, bending her head like a chastised child. But she didn't refute her words, or offer him a graceful way to reject her. She just said, so softly he had to strain to hear her, "I do mean it, Peter. I do."

Holy Heaven, what did he do now? "Thea, I never meant for you to think I'd take advantage of your situation, that I'd try to take advantage of you." But he had taken advantage, he realized. Just by pushing for this marriage, just by asking her to view him as her hero. "If I gave you the idea that I expected..." He fumbled for words. "I don't want you to think I expected you to...to offer yourself to me."

"This isn't about you, Peter. I know that...sex...has never entered your mind." A wisp of fleeting humor touched her lips and vanished. "Well, not in connection with me, anyway."

If it had never crossed his mind before, it was there now. And in his body, a stirring, a need to prove it. But he couldn't. She did not know what she was asking. "Thea, sex...well, it complicates things. And you should save yourself for, for..." Even as he said the words, though, even before she looked up at him and voiced his thoughts aloud, he understood.

"Save myself for what, Peter? The *right* husband? For *another* wedding night?" Her face was pale and earnest in the soft lamplight. "That isn't likely to happen for me, Peter. You know that as well as I do."

He opened his mouth to say it wasn't true, but she stopped him.

"Please don't offer some meaningless platitude about how it could happen, how I should be more optimistic and not give up hope of meeting Mr. Right. There was never much hope of that happening." She glanced away, looked resolutely back, despite the blush which cast her cheeks in a rosy embarrassment. "And I do know what I'm asking, Peter. I know you, I know *everyone* thinks I'm a virgin, but I'm...not."

Surprise hit him like a fist to the stomach, and spread outward in a confusing blend of disbelief and betrayal. And the oddest feeling of relief.

"I know you probably can't imagine that I, that any man would…" Her chin came up again, negating any protest he might try to make. "But I went to college, you know. I had…experiences."

"I'm glad to hear it," Peter said because what else the hell could he say?

"You are?" The flicker of confidence washed away as quickly as it had come and her hands twisted nervously. "It wasn't anything to write home about." She pulled at her lower lip with her teeth. "It was actually pretty awful. I mean, he was nice enough. At first. But then later…afterward, I found out it was a…a fraternity rite of passage. Or something like that."

Peter's fists clenched as his confusing feelings sharpened into anger. "Hazing?"

She couldn't meet his eyes. "Yes, I think so."

He had heard about dogfights, the so-called game of seducing the least attractive woman to be found and then comparing notes with other, equally insensitive, ignorant louts. He hadn't known it had reached the campuses of New England, but he shouldn't have been surprised. There were boys growing up in his stepfather's brutish image all over the world. But that one of them had harmed Thea's fragile heart seemed grossly unfair to him and brought back a sense of outrage and fury so deep its pain was almost cleansing. "If it would help, I'd track him down and beat him to a pulp for you.''

"I know you would, Peter," she said softly. "But I should have done that for myself. I could have reported him. I could have reported the whole fraternity, but he was from another state, a different college and I was…ashamed. I mean, I should have known better than to trust him. I should have known a good-looking, nice guy wouldn't want me for real.''

"He was not a *nice* guy, Thea."

Her sigh rushed out on waves of regret. "Listen, forget what I said. I shouldn't have asked, shouldn't have put you in such an awkward position." She sagged onto the bed, her hands falling limply into her lap, defeated. "Please, just go. I'll be all right. Ally is pretty good company.''

This was probably the wrong thing to do and it probably would only make matters worse for her. But Peter could not leave her thinking no man could ever desire her. Because it wasn't true. He desired her. His body had been quickening with that realization ever since this afternoon's kiss. Thea wasn't his type. He wasn't in love with her. But as surprising as it seemed, he was attracted to her. Probably, on some unconscious level, it was rooted in his new role as her protector, her rescuer. But that didn't change the fact that he wanted, more than anything, to show her what making love could, what it *should* be like.

Almost before he realized his intention—certainly before he thought it through—he was standing in front of her, reaching down to draw her to her feet, bending his head to discover once again the sweet innocence of her kiss.

"Peter…" She breathed his name in a quiet protest. "Please, don't…don't do this because you feel sorry for me. Please."

"Thea, believe me, pity is the very last thing I'm feeling." He made no attempt to mask the desire in his eyes, no attempt to conceal the hunger building inside him and which she would surely recognize as her body came into contact with his. "What I am feeling is a very real, very strong desire to make love to my wife."

She looked at him, searching for the truth in what he said, wanting to believe he meant it.

But he knew of only one way to prove it to her, so he gathered her into his arms and kissed her, full and forcefully, and with as much tender passion as he felt she could bear.

Chapter Eight

Thea didn't know what she had expected, but she hadn't thought Peter would kiss her. Or hold her. Or even be particularly subtle in refusing her request. She hadn't had even an imaginary hope he'd respond with such…enthusiasm. *A wedding night.* How could she have known he'd agree to that? And why had he? She'd said it partly because she hadn't liked his offering to keep her company, as if she were a child and needed someone to stay with her until she fell asleep. But mainly she'd said it because she needed to prove to her heart that Peter was a nice, good-looking guy who did not want her, either.

She knew there was a certain look in a man's eyes when he wanted a woman and recognized that she was willing. She had seen men look at her and decide they weren't that desperate. And that's what she had thought she would see in Peter's wonderful green eyes, too. That same, *no-thanks* expression. A flicker of distaste. A blink of amused surprise that she would think *he* could ever desire *her.*

But that is not what she'd seen.

She had seen the other look. The one that set the very air aquiver and lingered in the silence like music.

And now, his lips were coaxing her with kisses, as if he meant what he'd said.

And his arms held her tightly, as if he wanted her close against him.

And his hands. His hands caressed her, slowly, sweetly, as if she were a treasure to be handled with exquisite care.

Ambushed by his tenderness, blindsided by her own desire, Thea didn't know exactly what she'd expected, but she was oh, so glad she'd gotten this instead. If he suddenly stopped and pushed her away, realized what he was doing and with whom and rejected her outright, she'd still be grateful for this one glorious moment when he'd kissed her on purpose and with genuine passion. She didn't mind if he'd manufactured the emotion just for the occasion. She only cared that for now, for this one tiny handful of time, he wanted her.

Peter wanted her.

So she concentrated on the feel of his lips on hers and lost herself in a kiss that was so sweet it stole her breath away. She hadn't known a kiss could be so intensely soft, deliberately gentle and insistently sexual, all at the same time. She hadn't known a kiss could convey so much and still leave so much to be discovered. She hadn't known a kiss could make her wish for things she couldn't even name. But Peter's kiss upped the ante, sharpened her senses and turned time into one long, lovely loop of wonder. It was everything she'd ever imagined a passionate kiss might be, and nothing like she'd imagined at all. The other time, the first and only other time, there'd been few kisses and even less pleasure. Just a quick rush to fulfillment—his, not hers—and then it was over.

So this was her first time in every way that counted, and she determined to fall into the moment and savor every particle of it. Being this close to Peter was the best part, the passion in his kiss a close second, but then, to the sweet sensations of his mouth on hers, she added the fragrant scent of orchids, and the sluicing sound of water sprinklers coming on somewhere outside in the gardens. There was the feel of his arms warm and strong around her and the solid line of the mattress against the backs of her thighs. Inside her, there was the crescendo of her own erratic pulse, and beneath her palm, there was the hard, fast rhythm of Peter's beating heart. *Ka-thud. Ka-thud. Ka-thud.*

She wanted to be able to remember these moments, these kisses, when she was alone again and memory was all she had. Tonight with Peter might be the most she ever tasted of pleasure, all she ever learned about a man's desire. She had to live it all and remember it well. She had to dive into the experience with a whole heart and a brave spirit.

Tentatively, because she wasn't sure what was allowed and what wasn't, she slid her hands up and around his neck, nestled closer, parted her lips and waited to see what happened.

And what happened was that he gathered her in like a much-needed rain—one hand moving to cup the back of her head, one hand settling firmly in the curve of her spine—and drew her deeper into the embrace, tucking her pliant body into the hard contours of his. His tongue laved the inner outline of her lips and when she caught her breath in surprise at the heat that one simple act ignited inside her, he took advantage and plunged deeper into her mouth, turning the kiss from pure pleasure into a sweeping and carnal hunger.

Thea hadn't known it was possible to feel such a primal need. She'd never been touched like this, never suspected desire could be so exquisitely painful. She had always thought making love would be like jumping into an abyss, one wild impulsive leap and a fast, frantic fall into fulfillment. Her one jump into sex had been impulsive, fast, frantic and wildly unfulfilling. She'd been disappointed even before it was over and long before she discovered the betrayal. But it would not be like that with Peter. He would make love to her the way it should be made, give her this gift of memory so she wouldn't have to wonder ever again.

Thea kissed him back, deciding if this was her only chance, she would learn all she could, memorize every angle and slope and line of his body, investigate his taste and his texture, explore the ways he incited her response and figure out, perhaps, what she could do to evoke his. She would connect the dots of him and make for herself a lovely fantasy that she could call up whenever she wanted to remember what love felt like.

Peter eased the pressure, pulling his lips from hers, only to feather kisses along her jaw to the hollow of her ear and down to the hollows of her throat. She arched her neck, trying to feel each of the shivery sensations in turn, trying to hold on to the delicious phenomena as long as possible. But each touch was new and set her on fire in a different way. How that was possible, she didn't know, didn't particularly care. She simply wanted him never to stop touching her, never to stop making love to her.

He trailed kisses across her shoulder and wove his fingers into her hair, giving an almost painful tug against the pins, which somehow felt good, too. It was too much for one person to feel and she gave up trying to hold it all and let the crystalline fires burn what they would into her memory. She had never felt so good. Nothing had ever felt so good. Night and day, fire and rain, it all made sense to her now, was somehow all a part of Peter's kiss, a part of what she felt for him. *Please,* she prayed to whatever gods would heed her. *Please, don't let this end too soon.*

Without any conscious intent, her hands traveled the muscular breadth of his shoulders, found the smoothness of his jaw and cupped his face within her palms, stopping the nuzzling kisses herself and bringing his face back to hers. "Peter," she whispered because she wanted to feel his name on her lips and mark it indelibly on her heart.

"Thea," he whispered back, but there was a question in his eyes and hesitation in his voice. "Are you sure? We don't have to take this any further."

"Yes, we do. Please, Peter, show me. Show me what love is like."

His jaw tensed against her palm and then he put his hands over hers and drew them down from his face, holding them within the shelter of his large hands, placing a gentle, fiercely exciting kiss on each of her wrists in turn, never taking his gaze from hers or allowing her gaze to wander from his. As if she wanted to look at anything else. As if she wouldn't be content to stare into his eyes for the rest of her life.

"Your eyes are so brown they're almost black," he said as if the discovery had been worth the wait. "I never knew that before. You've been hiding them behind those glasses."

True.

"You hide your body, too, don't you, Thea?"

She nodded, because that, too, was true.

"Why is that, Thea? What are you hiding from? Who are you hiding from?"

But she could not answer, could not speak, could not tell him she had been hiding for so long she was afraid there was not enough left of her for anyone to find.

"Don't hide from me, Thea. I won't hurt you. Let me see you tonight."

She was willing. She was more than willing. And so very afraid he would find nothing in her to see.

But she'd discovered a vein of courage today and

she tapped it one more time. "Show me what to do, Peter, and I'll...I'll try to please you."

He shook his head, bringing his hands back to her face, cupping, cradling her face and stroking her cheeks with his thumbs. "Tonight, Thea, I will please you."

Then he bent to her again, his lips breaching the distance in a slow deliberate motion, touching and teasing and tasting her with his kiss until she was pulled up on tiptoe by the tension to kiss him back, to open her mouth and invite him in. She followed his lead as boldly as she knew how, touching her tongue to the corners of his mouth, sucking lightly on his lower lip. He groaned softly and the ache inside her became an emptiness that throbbed low in her belly, robbing her of fear, revealing a streak of truly wanton desire. She wanted this more than anything. She would have it or die.

His hand slid like satin from her nape to her neck and down the bare slope of skin to brush across the top of her breast. She shivered as her nipples peaked with anticipation. If he'd touch her there, it would be enough. But when his fingers slipped inside the folds of silk fabric and tugged at her breast, she knew how foolish the thought had been. As if the erotic pull on her nipple would be enough. She wanted more. She wanted to rip the wedding dress, to feel it fall from her like too many inhibitions. She wanted to bare her body to his view and her soul to his. She wanted to touch his skin, massage it, kiss it. She wanted to take him inside of herself and make love to him as best she knew how.

But even as the need grew within her, she felt him pulling away, taking his hand from her breast to put it on her shoulder, so he could turn her gently away. "I don't want to tear your dress," he said as if it mattered. Before she could tell him it didn't, his fingers had already begun the unbuttoning, and the material was already drooping, sliding, falling across her shoulders, down her arms, over her breasts, to her waist, and pooling like moonlight around her feet. His breath caressed the back of her neck, the curve of her shoulder, and the series of kisses he left there sent shivers racing in so many directions she was amazed they all came to rest in the same low center core of her body. He explored the slope of her neck, his tongue tracing the path to the hollows behind her ear and she caught her breath lest just the act of breathing might stop him from doing more.

"Give me a minute," he whispered softly into her ear and she felt his absence immediately. What if he didn't come back? Where was he going? Could she do something to stop him?

She turned in time to see him close the door...and lock it. He smiled at her then and she trembled at the realization of how handsome he was and how special he was and how little she had to offer in return. But he shrugged out of his jacket, tugged off his shoes, and jerked off his socks, and she was mesmerized by the efficiency of his movements, by the sheer masculine appeal of them. He stripped off his black tie, and began unbuttoning the crisp, tucked shirt that gleamed white against his skin. And all the while, he smiled at her. A good smile. A tender smile. A smile that meant something.

It wasn't until he unfastened the studs at his wrists and tossed them onto the dressing table, that he walked back to her, the shirt hanging open to show a strip of muscled chest and the thin cloud of dark curls that covered it.

Thea swallowed hard, unaware until the moment he stopped in front of her, that she'd been standing before him in nothing more than a strip of lace underpants and a push-up bra. At that moment, her first thought was that she owed Ainsley Danville a huge debt of gratitude that she, Thea, wasn't standing before her new husband wearing underwear more serviceable than seductive. But her second thought, coming right on top of the first, was that Peter was looking at her with something very akin to admiration, and maybe—just maybe—it would be okay that she hadn't thought to turn out the lights.

His smile softened, but didn't go away. "Could you help me with my shirt?" he asked, sending her heartbeat ricocheting from fast to speedy and back again.

She couldn't speak. She inhaled sharply and shoved her hands beneath the pleated cotton, surprised by the heat that met her palms, by the sensual texture of his skin and by the cool slick feel of the shirt. It was too late for him to turn and run. She'd tackle him if she had to, but there was no way she could let him go now that she knew the feel of him. Without considering how a woman went about undressing a man, she pushed the shirt up and off his shoulders and soaked in the perfection of him with her eyes and with the flexing of her fingers. "Oh," she whispered, awestruck, her gaze flicking upward to his, then falling again to his chest.

His pleasure rumbled beneath her fingertips...not quite a laugh, not quite a sigh. And then he pushed aside the push-up cup and folded his hand around her breast, bringing the ache and the heat and the need back to life with a mere touch. "You have a beautiful body, Thea."

She hugged the compliment to herself, adding it to her treasure trove of memories, telling herself he meant it for the moment. And the moment, after all, was all that counted. "So do you," she said in a breathy rush.

"I want to make love to you now."

Searching his eyes, she saw nothing but truth and passion and desire. "I might die if you don't," she answered.

The slow release of air from his lungs revealed something she hadn't expected. He shared this trembling anticipation, this agony of waiting that held both ecstasy and anguish. He did want her. She would live on the sweetness of that knowledge for the rest of her life. Peter wanted her.

She kissed him then, his chest, his nipples, his neck, his shoulders, his chin. She loved him with her lips and with her touch and exulted in every kiss and every touch he returned to her. When he got rid of the bra, she banished the impulse to feel embarrassed and faced him with her shoulders back, her chin lifting, her breasts bare. He smiled and said again, "Beautiful."

Just the one word, and she took that in, too, holding it tightly in her heart. She didn't know how she found the courage to slip her thumbs into the sides of her panties and slide them off, but she did. And she thought, perhaps, it would be all right with him if she did the same to his briefs, but her brazen bravery deserted her and he did it himself. For which she was grateful because it afforded her the chance to see that he hadn't been lying. He did, indeed, desire her. His body was thick and hard with the evidence and her blush sprang, hot and high, into her cheeks.

He took her into his arms then and held her close, kissing her temple, her eyelids, easing her into acceptance of this new state of being, this moment when they were both naked and new to the other. When he lifted her in his arms and laid her on the bed, she sank into the miracle of what was happening.

But as he settled in beside her, she stopped thinking about the *what* and just let the wonder of it happen. He would be gentle, tender, but he would not withhold his passion, either. She knew, somehow, he would make love to her in a way he had never made love before to any other woman. He would give her all of himself for this, her wedding night. And she would give him all she knew to give back.

Her heart. Her breath. Her life. Her love.

It seemed the least she could offer.

Peter lay awake long after Thea had fallen asleep.

They'd talked softly for a long time. Well, mostly, she'd talked, hesitantly at first, as if it were a new experience to have someone listen. He'd been content to ask a question here and there and hear the quiet pleasure in her voice as she responded to his interest. With a little encouragement, she talked about her pets, current and past, about the day she figured out she could climb a tree, about the first time she picked up a sketchpad and knew she'd found a friend, about Monroe and his wife, Sadie, about the little everyday somethings that made up her life. Eventually, though, she drifted into sleep, fighting it all the way, still talking, sentences dissolving into fragments and disconnected words, but then finally succumbing to slumber like an exhausted child, overcome at last by the events of a long day.

And he lay awake, watching her, wondering about this odd little person who he'd rescued and made his wife. Her hair was tousled, the topknot intact, but all askew, a fuzzy mess of pins that stuck out at odd angles against the pillow, curls that no longer curled, and one forlorn sprig of baby's breath snared deep in the tangle. One wispy strand had fanned across her face, a straggle caught in her eyebrow, another entwined with her lashes, the flyaway ends fluttered near the corner of her mouth.

Carefully, so as not to disturb her, he untangled the strand and tucked it behind her ear, allowing his fingers to brush her cheek in a fleeting caress. And just in that simple gesture, a fierce pride welled up inside him all over again. Why he should feel so proud of himself for marrying her he didn't quite understand. There were problems ahead, legalities to be sorted out, and Peter wasn't foolish enough to think Davinia had been defeated. She would try to get her granddaughter back and crush him in the process, if she could. But she couldn't hurt him. He was a Braddock. Besides, he was willing to go down in flames to keep her away from his wife. The only way Thea was ever going back to Grace Place was over his dead body. She deserved a life of her own, and Peter meant to give it to her.

With a quiet sigh, he drew his hand away from his disheveled bride, thinking that even in sleep, she was curled into herself, knees pulled up, arms tucked close to her body, hands folded under her chin, as if she feared encroaching into his personal space while she slept.

Too late.

She was in his space, no matter where she stayed in this bed. He'd made love to her. To Thea. His wife. Not just once, either, but until they both were sated with satisfaction and blissfully weary. Even now his body quickened with the possibility of loving her yet again. He hadn't thought he could desire her so or that she would be such an adventurous, enthusiastic lover. Certainly, she'd surprised him over and over with her eagerness to learn, her desire to please him, her delight in discovering how he could please her. All in all, her wedding night had turned out to be a whole lot more than he'd expected.

Peter knew this marriage of convenience would come to an end. Eventually, Thea would gain all the confidence she needed to make her own decisions without help from him or anyone else. But for now, he planned to do everything in his power to prove to her she was worth the effort. She could be, was already, in fact, a desirable woman and he was determined that before long everyone else would know it, too. All she needed was a little guidance, an infusion of self-assurance, someone to listen to her, someone who cared.

The annual Harvest Gala benefit was coming up at the end of the month, barely two weeks from now. It was one of the biggest events of the year, the highlight of the fall season. That, Peter decided, would be Thea's debut as a woman of fashion and substance. Well, she already had the substance—more, really, than any of the pretty debutantes he'd fancied—but she needed to show some style to fit in with this crowd. With the right clothes, a little makeup and a good haircut, Thea would be the talk of the town. He smiled just thinking of how proud she'd be to finally get the attention she deserved. Her peers, the society to which she had every blue-blooded right to belong, owed her that attention and a long overdue respect.

She sighed in her sleep, murmured something unintelligible, but oddly contented, and his lips curved with a tender smile. In a way, he hated to have to share her with anyone else. But he couldn't stand in her way. She'd married him to escape a bad situation at home.

He'd married her solely to give her this opportunity…and she was going to have it or else. He'd need to exercise considerable diplomacy in making suggestions though. He didn't want her to think he believed there was anything wrong with her just the way she was. Because there wasn't. Not really. She just needed someone to give her that initial boost of confidence and courage, a healthy measure of approval. Then he was convinced it'd be, *watch out, world, here she comes!*

He yawned, oddly at peace with himself in a way he hadn't been for a long time. Perhaps, never. Certainly, not since his mother had died and he'd found out that James Braddock was truly his father and that Braddock Hall would be his new home. He felt guilty at times that his life had turned out so well and his sister, Briana, had been left with her father, the man Peter had believed for nine years was his father, too. James had tried to help Briana, then. Peter had tried to help her since, but she'd made her choices, just as he'd made his, and there could be no going back.

Thea's foot brushed his beneath the covers, sending a quicksilver burst of desire to his groin. He turned onto his side, making further such contacts less likely, knowing he ought to leave and let Thea have the bed to herself. There would be no more lovemaking tonight. She needed her rest. So did he. But he continued to lie there for the longest time, just watching her breathe, smiling a little at the expressions that flitted from time to time across her face, remembering how sweet she'd looked as she walked into the library this afternoon in her new, old-fashioned gown, how his heart had stopped when she fainted. Not the way he'd pictured his wedding at all, yet perfect in a way he couldn't describe even to himself.

His eyelids drifted down and he pushed them open again, telling himself to get up and go to his own bed in his own room. It was one of the rules he'd always lived by, leave before there was ever a question of staying. That had saved him from those awkward mornings after and spared him any pretense of commitment. This was the first time, too, that his bedroom was close enough to walk to without having to get in a car and drive home first. So he had no excuse. It ought to be easy. Get up. Walk back to his room. Go to bed.

But he hated to leave her all the way over here on the other side of the house. And, knowing Thea, if she awoke alone, she'd jump to all the wrong conclusions about why he'd gone to sleep in his own room. She'd think she'd done something wrong, kept him awake, or that he simply hadn't wanted to stay. The truth was he did want to stay. The bed was warm and the sound of her breathing comforted him like a heartbeat. And, where was the harm? He'd married her, and that was more commitment than he'd ever made to anyone, even if both he and Thea knew love and forever were not a part of the bargain.

Peter inhaled, sleepily, and made his decision. She had asked for a wedding night and, technically, the night lasted until morning.

He would stay.

She woke him three times before dawn. Once by accident, twice by design. She apologized the first time, but not the other two.

It was, all things considered, a pretty great way to spend any night, even if neither of them got all that much sleep.

THEA TRIED TO BE stealthy as she picked Peter's tuxedo shirt up off the floor, slipped it over her bare shoulders and wrapped the flappy sleeves around her in a starchy hug. She loved the bigness of his shirt, the way it fell halfway to her knees, the crisp feel of the fabric and its lingering scent of soap and cologne and man. She loved the whole world this morning and wouldn't, at that moment, have traded her life for anyone's. Well, maybe with the beautiful blonde who was somewhere out there and who would, someday, be Peter's wife for real. But she wasn't going to think about things like that this morning, not when her body was deliciously sore from his lovemaking, not when the sun was just peeking over the horizon and edging into the room through the window, tinting the calico ball that was Ally, who was asleep on the window seat, in rose-gold hues.

Dancing on her toes, Thea pliéd into the bathroom, squinching her eyes shut so she wouldn't accidentally catch a glimpse of herself in the mirror and lose the fantasy. That could ruin a promising morning. Come to think of it, she probably ought to close the drapes.

She'd barely danced her way out of the bathroom and over to the window to check on the sun's progress, when she heard the rustle of bedcovers and looked over her shoulder to see Peter smiling at her. ''You look cute,'' he said, his voice hazy with sleep.

Cute? He must not have his eyes all the way open

yet. Or maybe he thought she was someone else. Or maybe that was the kind of thing men said to women on the morning after, whether they meant it or not. But as no one had ever said *"you look cute"* to her before on any occasion, Thea decided to accept the compliment graciously. "I'm wearing your shirt," she said as if that explained it.

"If you take it off, I'll give you a kiss."

A bribe. That was the best thing anyone had ever offered her this early in the morning. Ever. "Just a kiss?" she asked to make sure he knew she wasn't impressed.

"Okay, Vixen, name your price."

Vixen? Maybe he was talking in his sleep. And how could she tell him what she wanted now that the wedding night she'd requested was technically over? "I can't give the shirt back," she said, thinking fast. "I haven't anything else to wear."

His smile edged into a grin and he pushed up onto his elbow. The sheet slipped from his shoulder and folded in about his waist and Thea's knees got weak at the sight of so much man, so early in the day. "I don't see the problem," he said, and patted the empty place beside him. "Come back to bed."

No need to ask her twice. She was nestled in next to him before he had a chance to rethink his original idea. "Now, what?" she asked, hoping he'd kiss her and put her out of her misery. Except that she didn't feel the least bit miserable.

"You forgot to take off the shirt," he said, but he kissed her anyway.

"I HAVE AN IDEA."

Thea thought he'd had several in the last hour. All of them spectacularly good. "Will I like it as much as the last one?"

He laughed, a low rumble beneath her head, which rested on his bare chest as she lay cradled against his side. "Maybe more. It involves shopping."

"I don't like shopping."

"You don't?"

"Not for clothes." She wished she hadn't said that. Now she'd have to admit that shopping was a frustrating, humiliating experience and she did not like to do it. "I like shopping for art supplies."

"But you don't need art supplies and at some point in the very near future, you're going to need something to wear."

She sighed. "Can't I just stay in this bedroom forever?"

"Not if you want to be with me." He brushed his fingertips across her forehead, probably trying to lift some of her wild hair out of her eyes. "Trust me," he said, "you'll like the kind of shopping I have in mind."

She knew she wouldn't, but she did want to be with him and if the only way for that to occur was to shop, well, then, she'd shop. "How soon do we have to go?"

"How about now?"

"What will be open at..." She glanced at the clock on the bedside table. "six-twenty in the morning?"

"Thea, Thea." His voice rumbled beneath her head with good humor. "When you spend the kind of cash we're about to spend, believe me, getting someone to open the store isn't a problem.''

"Oh," she said. "So there probably won't be many other shoppers there?"

"Just you and me. And a few very lucky merchandisers.''

That didn't sound too bad. Except, of course, that Peter would be disappointed when he saw how badly she looked in the clothes. No matter how much they cost. "Could we put this off until later in the week, when I'm a little more...rested?"

"Today's the only day I have free, Thea. It has to be today. Unless you'd rather go with Katie. Although, I don't think she's much of a shopper, either. And Lara will be working. What about Mrs. Fairchild? Or Ainsley Danville? Would you rather go with one of them?"

"No. I'd rather spend the day with you. Even if I have to spend it shopping."

He laughed then with genuine affection in his voice. "Thea Braddock," he said. "You are one of a kind."

Thea Braddock. She was Thea *Braddock.*

At least for today.

And today her husband wanted to take her shopping.

"Can I wear your shirt to the store?" she asked, actually sort of hoping he'd say yes.

"No," he answered. "I'd never be able to keep my hands off of you."

Even if he was just being nice, she thought that was just about the best thing he could have said. She rubbed her head against his chest. "Then I don't see the problem."

"The problem would come when I took the shirt off of you in the store, scandalizing the sales associates."

"Oh, well, in that case, I think I will wear it."

"You know, Thea, with the right encouragement, I believe you could set society in the little state of Rhode Island right on its collective ear."

She had already done that by marrying him, the most eligible bachelor in New England and, in her opinion, the handsomest and best of the famous Braddock brothers. She imagined there would be quite a few shocked expressions and rampant speculation around Rhode Island's breakfast tables as the news traveled out...as news always did.

But she didn't say that to Peter.

She just laughed and eventually, allowed him to coax her out of bed with the promise that they'd slip out of the house together, thereby avoiding the rest of the family, and eliminating the need to tell anyone where they were going.

Chapter Nine

"This color will look fabulous on you, Mrs. Braddock."

"That dress is just your style, Mrs. Braddock."

"With your figure, you can wear anything, Mrs. Braddock."

Thea had never had so many people wanting to help her. She'd never gotten this kind of attention, in or out of a store. She'd never had so many luscious fabrics and rich colors draped on her body. She'd never known there were so many beautiful clothes in the world, much less in one place. Before she could get even a good look at herself in one outfit, it was whisked away and replaced with another.

"Try this sweater with that skirt, Mrs. Braddock."

"Let's see what these shoes do for that ensemble, Mrs. Braddock."

"Definitely this handbag with that outfit, Mrs. Braddock."

"Great legs, Mrs. Braddock."

That last from Peter, who grinned at her as she was

spun for his approval and whisked off for yet another outfit and accessory change. He seemed to be delighted with the attention she was receiving and with the way she looked. Thea tried to see something different when she looked at herself in the mirror, but she didn't know what colors looked good on her and she had no idea what her style was, so she tried on garment after garment, modeling everything for Peter, taking his nod for yes, his shrug for no. And when finally the shopping was over and she was walking out of the store in one complete head-to-toe outfit while the rest were being steamed or altered or wrapped up for later delivery, Thea was the weary owner of more new clothes than she had ever possessed in all of her life.

"You should do this every day for a month." Peter took her hand in his, swinging it a little as they walked toward the car. "Just to get the hang of it."

"Every *day?*" She was horrified at the thought of having to set foot in a store again anytime soon.

He laughed and teased her with a squeeze of her hand. "Oh, come on, Thea, it wasn't that bad. And you look fabulous."

She felt uncomfortable in the short-skirted jacket dress she was wearing. She felt self-conscious in the bright autumn-red color. She felt awkward and ungainly in the unaccustomed high heels she'd been told she absolutely had to have to go with this classic fall ensemble. The gold earrings pinched her ears. The beautiful alpaca wool shawl kept slipping from its artful drape about her shoulders. The designer hat was too tight and she longed to take it off, although she knew that would defeat its purpose, which was to keep her unsightly hair out of sight. But if Peter liked the way she looked, then she'd learn to like all these fashion discomforts. As long as he smiled at her and held her hand, then what kind of idiot would she be to complain?

SHE LOVED his Boston office.

Peter could tell by the way she trailed her fingertips over the rich, dark wood of his desk. He could tell by the delighted approval in her eyes as she looked around the big corner office. He could tell by the soft tug of a smile on her lips that she was pleased he'd furnished his professional lair with fine antiques and old architectural drawings. He could tell by her soft, *"ohs"* of surprise that she'd expected a less traditional look, something trendier and more modern, something with more glass and less charm.

He was pleased when she paused to study his early model of the Atlanta project and when she took the time to read the newspaper article about it. He liked the way she tipped her head to the side as she looked at each of his awards in turn. He loved the serious little frown that gathered across her brow as she silently, but obviously, counted up the total. It was an impressive array, he knew, even for someone with his name and family connections. Peter was proud of his achievements, and that he'd chosen this career field. It had, in one fell swoop, secured a common interest with Braddock Industries, while giving him an area of expertise not already overshadowed by his two older brothers. And in some way, Peter felt that in the planning and designing of buildings, he could pay homage to the dreams his mother had nurtured for him. She had wanted him to build a better life than she thought she could give him and he felt she would have been proud of him for the life he had made.

He sometimes wondered how his life might have turned out if she hadn't been so intent on his claiming his true heritage, his place as a Braddock. But then, if she'd only had the courage to leave her husband, she might still be alive. He and his sister might have finished their growing up at Braddock Hall with their mother, instead of being separated and growing up apart with two different views of what had happened to them.

"You're an artist, Peter." Thea glanced at him before returning her attention to four, small, framed sketches above his work station. "These are wonderful."

In the Sunday stillness of his office, with the whole building mostly deserted and quiet around them, he felt a thrill that she'd noticed the four pieces of which he was most proud.

"Is that your mother?"

He nodded and walked over to stand beside her and look at the pencil drawings. "Catherine Latiker. She was never a Braddock because she was already married when she met my father."

"She was very beautiful." Thea looked at the others. "And that one?" she asked, indicating the drawing of a little girl with a crooked smile and a spattering of freckles across her nose.

"My sister. Half sister. Briana. She's older now, of course, nearly thirty, but that's her at the age I remember best."

"A sister," Thea said with a wistful sigh. "I always wished I might have had a sister. Do you get to see her often?"

"Hardly ever. After our mother died, James came for me and Briana stayed with *him*." Peter nodded at the third picture in the grouping. "My stepfather. I keep him there to remind me that sometimes the truth we tell ourselves is the biggest lie of all. My mother should have left him before it was too late. She could have. She just didn't."

He felt Thea's eyes on him and wondered why he'd said that. He'd only ever told his Grandmother Jane why he'd drawn that picture and why he kept it there. "And the last drawing is, of course, my grandmother. I sketched out all of these my first year at Harvard. They're not great art, but I love them just the same."

"That's what art is, Peter. Emotion on paper. A way to draw feelings." She looked up at him with a smile. "And you certainly captured your feelings in these sketches."

He smiled back because she understood what he'd been trying to say. He smiled because she was easy company, undemanding and thoughtful. He smiled because she looked cute and funny in the new clothes. She'd ripped off the hat the minute they'd walked through his office door and her hair had sprawled out in its usual, ragtag fashion. She'd dropped the shawl across the back of one of the chairs, where it had promptly slid to the floor, unnoticed, of course, by Thea. She'd pulled off the gold earrings and carried them around in her palm, clinking them one over the other without being aware she was doing so. Peter thought the new clothes were a considerable improvement, even if she did wear them with no measurable increase in confidence. But he was on the right track with Thea. She just needed a little more encouragement.

"I like your new clothes," he said and was disappointed when the frown returned to her brow and she looked down, her fingers plucking at the dress.

"You don't think this is too...red?" she asked, clearly uncertain.

"It's perfect, Thea. Trust me." It wasn't exactly perfect, but she needed color in her life and he'd thought clothes were a good place to start. "Now that you've seen my office, what else would you like to do?"

Her smile returned like the promise of spring and he thought maybe the clothes had made a difference after all because she looked...pretty. "Don't you have an apartment here in Boston?"

"Several whole apartment complexes, as it happens," he said. "But one apartment that I keep for my own personal use. As a matter of fact, it's within walk-

ing distance of the Commons and this very office building.''

"Now *that* is what I consider good planning, Peter.''

He didn't know how meek, shy little Theadosia Berenson had become saucy and seductive Thea Braddock
over the course of one wedding night, but he figured
there were some things about her he didn't need to
understand to appreciate.

"If that's where you want to spend the afternoon,
Mrs. Braddock, then grab your hat, get your shawl, put
your earrings back on and off we'll go.''

She seemed a tad reluctant to comply, but she did it
anyway.

ILSA WALKED INTO Neath's bistro five minutes late and
forty-eight hours flustered. "I'm here to meet James
Braddock,'' she said to the maitre d' who greeted her.

With a smile and a bow, he led her straight to where
James was seated at a table with a view of the Providence riverfront. He rose at her approach, all charming
welcome and handsome smile, and she promptly forgot
everything she'd told herself about how this was a casual dinner with an old friend, nothing to be nervous
about, nothing to lose sleep over.

James Braddock meant to court her.

Ilsa knew that in every granule of her matchmaker's
heart and the knowledge showed in the nervous flutter
of a smile she offered as she took her seat and he settled back into his. "I'm late,'' she confessed, as if,

perhaps, he might believe that was the reason for her breathiness.

"I would have waited a lifetime," he said, which didn't help. "Maybe I already have."

Nothing like skipping the preliminaries and dipping straight into the main event, Ilsa thought, but she was determined to get this on a more comfortable footing. If he kept looking at her like that, she'd never be able to eat a bite of her dinner—a sure indicator of heart problems and not the sort medical science could cure, either. "In that case, you must be very hungry."

She picked up the menu, holding it firmly in case the shaking going on inside her transmitted itself to her fingers. James had always been able to fluster her, even when they were both married to someone else. It had been innocent then. It wasn't now. She had been mentally listing all the reasons not to get involved with him ever since he'd made this dinner date a week ago.

One—he was a bad risk for any heart to take.

Two—he'd been married and divorced more times than she cared to know.

Three—he was just a couple of months out of his last relationship, an engagement to a woman almost half his age.

Four—he had three sons by three different women and although there had been mitigating circumstances in each of those three relationships, they didn't alter the fact that he wouldn't win any prizes for his parenting abilities.

Five—he would never make it past the rather stringent criteria she set for her clients.

In other words, James Braddock was without a doubt the handsomest, most charming man of her acquaintance and she still would advise any woman who asked her advice about getting involved with him to run as fast as she could in the opposite direction.

So what had *she* done when push came to shove?

She'd accepted his invitation to dinner and spent the entire day in a tizzy of anticipation that would have embarrassed even a lovestruck teen. Ainsley had been no help at all, either, when she'd finally wheedled the information out of Ilsa late this afternoon.

"You have a *date* with Mr. Braddock?" she'd said, all tactless youth and callow surprise. "Wow, you'd better be careful, Mrs. Fairchild. I'm not sure you can handle him. It's a good thing you're too old to have sex."

Ilsa had come very close to firing her apprentice then and there, but she'd actually done something much worse. She'd declared rather hotly that she not only *wasn't* too old to have sex, she *enjoyed* having it on a regular basis. Which was, of course, a bald-faced lie and played perfectly into Ainsley's devious little plans.

"Oh," the little snip had said then with a mischievous grin. "Then be sure to take along some protection in case tonight turns out to be an *enjoyable* evening for both you and Mr. Braddock."

Ilsa's nervousness had increased tenfold from that point on, throwing her off her normal stride, leaving her jumpy and putting sex smack dab in the middle of this cozy little table, instead of in some far off never-never land where it belonged.

"Are you ready?" James asked and she slammed the menu shut as if he'd shot her.

"No." It came out uncertain and tremulous, not at all like her usual calm, self-assured voice. "No," she repeated, without any noticeable improvement.

"Take your time," he said, looking a little concerned. "We have all night."

Ilsa grabbed for her composure and got it firmly in tow. She had decided to have dinner with James. She *wanted* to have dinner with him. And while she was not too old to have sex, she was thankfully past the age where it had to be the central question around which every enjoyable evening revolved. "Let's have some wine before we order," she said, in a calmer tone which translated into a calmer feeling. "And you can tell me what's been going on at the Hall."

"If you're asking about the newlyweds, we haven't seen them in three days. Not since the wedding."

"Really?" That was definitely a surprising development. "I didn't think Peter had planned a honeymoon trip."

"He didn't. At least, not any that he mentioned. He and Thea disappeared sometime early Sunday morning. They're in Boston, but the only reason we know that is because Peter called in from his office and talked to Lara at the Providence office. She said he talked mostly about the project he's working on, but he did say he and Thea had been shopping."

"Shopping," Ilsa repeated, pondering the implications. "Hmm. Do you think…" But she stopped herself before it could become rank speculation, a futile exercise she usually managed to avoid. "I hope they're having a lovely time together."

He lifted an eyebrow, opened the wine list, and said, "I don't think that's very likely, do you, Ilsa?"

She thought about it while he ordered a carafe of wine. When the waiter was gone and James looked at her for an answer, she smiled, back finally on solid emotional footing. "I believe, James, there are possibilities in every relationship that even I can't imagine."

"I sincerely hope so, Ilsa," he said, turning the conversation instantly intimate and very personal. "I most sincerely hope so." His smile was dangerously seductive, and her response to the challenge in it was a rather youthful thrill of discovery.

When the wine arrived, he tipped his glass to hers and made a toast. "To the possibility, then, that this is merely the first of many evenings you and I will spend together."

"The first of many *enjoyable* evenings," Ilsa said and clinked her glass to his in celebration.

IT WAS THE BEST TIME Thea had ever had. The best days. The best nights. The best week. The best time. Ever.

She made Peter breakfast every morning, which surprised him nearly as much as it did her. But she knew how to cook. She'd spent more time with Sadie and Monroe in the kitchen at Grace Place than she'd ever spent with friends her own age. "You don't have to do this, Thea," Peter had said the first day. "We have a very expensive chef on staff at the office. He has nothing to do but cook."

But she loved the wifely thrill of getting out of bed while he was still in the shower and setting plates on the table, putting toast in the toaster and pouring two glasses of juice. One for him. One for her. And she loved watching him sit at the table in his suit, with his tie perfectly knotted, his shirt perfectly starched and his jacket draped over the back of the chair. She loved when he downed the last swallow of juice and rose to leave, brushing her lips at the door, murmuring an already distracted, "See you tonight." She loved when the door closed behind him and she was alone in the apartment with his things. She loved cleaning the kitchen and remembering with dazzling satisfaction all she and Peter did together when he was home to keep her company.

The days idled by while she sketched people and pets on the Commons and walked away the chill of autumn. She had lunch with Peter twice during the week, meeting him at a sandwich shop near his office, listening while he talked about the work that absorbed his daytime hours. She shopped, too, but only because she knew he would ask, "What did you buy today?" And she'd always have something bright and colorful to show him, something she'd bought because she thought he'd like it, not because she particularly did.

She wore his clothes more than her own, loving the feel of his shirtsleeves on her arms, the novelty of having so much masculinity surrounding her. She knew the clothes he'd chosen for her were a big improvement over anything she'd ever worn in the past, and she wore them whenever she went out. But she still felt like an impostor in them, as if the wallflower she still was waited to jump out at her from every mirrored reflection.

Sometimes she put on the wedding gown, which she'd worn the morning they'd left as a matter of both convenience and necessity. She'd stand in front of the mirror in Peter's apartment and stare at the woman she saw reflected there to try to figure out what it was about the old-fashioned gown that made her feel strong and confident, that made her want to laugh aloud with pure delight at what she saw.

She did miss her cats and, though she'd never say so to Peter, she missed her grandmother, too. She knew the cats were well cared for at Braddock Hall because she asked and Abbott told her. She worried that Davinia might not be so fortunate at Grace Place. Of course, Monroe and Sadie were good to her and cared about her in their fashion, but Davinia Grace Carey wasn't the easiest person to love. And even if she didn't deserve it, Thea loved her.

Several times during that week, she'd started to pick up the phone to call Grace Place, let Monroe and Sadie and Davinia know she was happy, and perhaps, reassure her own heart that her grandmother was adjusting to life without her. But she didn't think Peter would like it. He talked sometimes as if she shouldn't want to have any contact with her former life, and she knew he'd already hired an attorney to start the process of breaking the trust or, at the very least, of removing Davinia as the trustee. Thea didn't care about the money, although she supposed she ought to want control of what was rightfully hers.

But she knew, even if Peter didn't, that having access to her fortune would not buy her one single piece of the happiness she had already found in simply being his wife.

And all the money in the world wouldn't prevent this, the best time of her life, from coming to its inevitable end.

"HELLO, LITTLE BROTHER."

Peter had had a feeling even before he picked up the phone that the person on the other end would be Bryce. He knew the family was wondering why he'd left the Hall Sunday morning without a word. He knew, too, they were mystified because he'd brought Thea to Boston with him. And kept her with him. He was a little surprised about that himself.

"Hello, yourself," he said, taking the opportunity to get up and stretch muscles that had been hunched over the work station for too many hours straight. "Let me guess. You're calling because you've had enough of that CEO's chair and think you may want a turn at my spot as lead architect.''

''Not even close.'' Bryce's voice was playful, as if he didn't have an ulterior motive, which Peter was certain he did. ''Can't a man call to talk to his brother without being accused of wanting some new responsibility? I'm ready for Adam to get back here permanently and take over this job any time he's ready, so believe me, I'm not angling for yours. Rumor is you'll be sitting in Vic Luttrell's seat when he retires next year and I say, hurrah for you. I certainly don't want to manage the whole Boston office. I'll be very happy heading up the new foundation and having a little extra time to teach my son all about sailing and other important things.''

''Calvin's already talking like a seasoned deckhand. He may wind up teaching you a few things about sailing…and other things.''

Bryce laughed. ''That would not surprise me. The kid has a memory like a sea sponge. Soaks up everything and repeats it verbatim as often as possible. Lara says he didn't get that quick wit from his biological parents, so it must be my influence.''

Peter loved the enthusiasm Bryce was bringing to his new role as a father. Without Lara's love and little Cal to guide him, he might never have found his own North Star. ''And you don't miss your old playboy days and ways?''

''Not in the least.'' There was only the slightest hesitation. ''What about you?''

Peter skirted the underlying question with a brisk, "There hasn't been time. I've been working every day."

"So where's Thea?"

"At the apartment, probably. Maybe out shopping. She's been doing a lot of that."

"Shopping, huh?"

"She's trying to get the hang of it, I think." She didn't seem to be enjoying it much, but Peter saw no reason to mention that.

"She's all right, then?"

He sometimes wished his brothers would just say flat out what was on their mind instead of ducking and weaving all around it. "She seems happy, but then who wouldn't be happy to be away from Davinia Carey?"

"Maybe she's just happy to be with you, Peter."

He caught the implication, but shrugged it aside as too much big brotherly concern. "Why wouldn't she be?" he asked, a grin in his voice. "I'm a nice guy...smarter *and* better-looking than either of my brothers."

Bryce didn't respond to the teasing tone. "You are a nice guy, Peter. That's why I hope you'll be careful with Thea. It's a big responsibility being someone's hero."

"Will you stop worrying about me?" he said, suddenly irritated by the inference. "I know what I'm doing."

"Okay, then. I'll worry about something else. Or I

would, if it was my nature to worry, which luckily, it isn't. How's the project coming?"

"I have that under control, too."

"Great. Gotta go, Bro. Nell is buzzing me. Allen is waiting to see me. I do not know why Adam loves this job. Will we see you and Thea at the Hall for Sunday dinner? Adam and Katie are taking off Monday morning for another month of high adventure—as Katie puts it. They won't be back again until Thanksgiving."

"We'll be at dinner Sunday," Peter said, even though the thought of taking Thea home, where all eyes would be on the two of them, made him decidedly uncomfortable.

"Great. See you then." Bryce hung up, leaving Peter with an uneasy, edgy feeling.

THE FEELING LINGERED through the weekend, through the trip with Thea back to Sea Change, and all the way through Sunday's dinner. Peter still felt unsettled even when they left the dining room and reassembled in the cozy, firelit library—Archer, James, Ilsa, three Braddock brothers and three Braddock wives. There had been nothing in the conversation, nothing in anyone's manner toward Thea that could have been considered the least bit objectionable. His wife was included into the family as naturally and as easily as he, himself, had been accepted as a nine-year-old boy. The camaraderie Peter shared with his brothers was a little teasing, a little affectionate and a little competitive, as it always was with Adam and Bryce. Katie and Lara accepted

Thea and chatted with her as easily as they talked with each other. Not a shred of disapproval met Peter's gaze, whether he was looking at his father, his grandfather or his brothers. But something pulled at him. There seemed to be something he should know, but didn't, something he should have done, but hadn't, something wrong that he needed to fix.

He couldn't get into the laughing conversation going on around him, the teasing that centered on Katie's yen to see Alaska in winter, and finally decided to write off this disquieting feeling as simple anxiety over the amount of work still remaining on the Boston project.

But then Thea looked over at him, catching his eye, and smiled a sweetly innocent and trusting smile.

His heart jerked and the unsettled feeling resolved itself into a startled awareness. He understood, suddenly, what his brothers had tried to warn him about, the danger he hadn't foreseen.

Thea was in love with him.

Chapter Ten

"If you need anything at all, Thea, just ask Abbott. I'm leaving the BMW convertible for you to drive, if you want. Or Benson will take you anywhere you want to go."

Except Boston.

Peter didn't say that, but Thea knew it, nonetheless. It was implicit in the way he stood just inside the bedroom, ill at ease and anxious to leave, looking everywhere but at her. It was clear in the unimportant things he was saying and in all the important things he was leaving unsaid. He hadn't even paused at the landing before turning toward the north ell of Braddock Hall, away from the family quarters, making her realize he didn't consider her one of the family, even if she was his wife. So she had turned with him, toward the guest wing and the suite he'd had decorated for her, the bedroom where they had spent their wedding night. She'd known, though, even before he stated it, that he was leaving.

And that she wasn't going with him.

Thea had known all along her little fantasy wouldn't last. She'd told herself to be grateful for every minute of it and to be ready when it was over to keep her chin up and face the future, knowing she'd already had more happiness in this temporary marriage than she'd ever expected to have in all of her life. And still, when she'd seen the way Peter had looked at her downstairs, as if he'd suddenly, finally, realized his mistake, her heart had jerked to a stop and she hadn't cared if it ever started beating again.

"I'll be back Saturday for the Harvest Gala," he said, as if the tension wasn't awkward and unwieldy, as if everything was still the way it was before. "You can shop all week, until you find the perfect dress to wear." His smile seemed forced, although the tender sadness in it was real enough. Peter was a gentleman. He'd never be cavalier about the end of their marriage, even if he was abruptly anxious to be free of the burden he'd taken on in making her his bride. "You could get your hair styled, too, Thea. I imagine Ainsley could tell you the best place to go in Providence. Of course, I'm not saying you should change it if you don't want to, just that you might want to try something different."

His voice ebbed fast and slow, trailing away at the end of his sentences as if he thought she might want to say something. But what was there to say? This wasn't her decision to make. None of the ones that mattered to her ever were. Holding back a sigh, she walked to the window seat and leaned down to stroke Ally's soft fur.

"It's better this way, Thea," he said sounding almost desperate. "I have to concentrate on the project this week and the fewer distractions I have, the better I can do that."

Ally stretched lazily beneath Thea's hand and began to purr.

"And I'm leaving for Boston now, tonight, so I can get an early start in the morning," he continued. "You do understand, don't you?"

More than she was ready to confess. But she didn't want to make this difficult for him. He'd never been hers to keep, anyway. This past week had simply been his way of trying to show her she could be a desirable woman, that she deserved more out of life, that she could be different. He'd meant her no harm. And she *had* asked him to show her what love was like. It wasn't his fault if she had learned a little more than he'd intended.

She looked up and offered him a ghost of a smile, which was the best she could manage under the circumstances. "I understand, Peter. Just go. I'll be all right." And she would. That was the good thing about never having much in the way of expectations. It was never a terrible shock when they failed to materialize. "Ally and the other cats and I will be fine."

But still he stood there, looking uncomfortable. "The attorney may need to talk to you this week. His name is Chip Hansen. There may be some papers for you to sign. About your trust.''

She nodded and continued petting the cat.

''Chip may ask you some questions about…about our marriage. You can tell him the truth.''

''What kind of questions?''

He met her curious gaze, looked quickly away. ''I think he may ask you if this is a…a real marriage. I told him that once the trust is broken, we'll want to have the marriage annulled and I, well, I believe he just assumed it hadn't been consummated.''

Thea felt a little like laughing because there probably wasn't a person who knew her and Peter who wouldn't assume the very same thing, who wouldn't be shocked to their marrow to find out otherwise. ''Does that make a difference?''

He shrugged. ''I don't think so. But I thought I should tell you the question probably will be asked.''

''Don't worry, Peter. I won't embarrass you.''

''Embarrass *me?* I was worried the question would embarrass you, Thea. I just didn't want Chip to surprise you, that's all.''

''All right,'' she said, her emotions shifting from that first giddy glee that her marriage *had* been consummated to the sobering reality that soon her marriage would be wiped from the records as if it had never been. A mistake acknowledged and forgotten by everyone except her. ''Wouldn't we have to get a…a divorce, if we told the truth?''

"I don't know. It might complicate things, but I don't think it would seriously affect the outcome."

And that was the bottom line. No matter who asked what question, no matter what she answered, the outcome would be the same. She would go back to being Thea Berenson again. As if she could ever be anyone else. "If Chip asks, I'll tell him the marriage was never consummated. I'm certain he'll believe me."

Peter hesitated, started to say something else, then seemed to let it go. "So I'll see you Saturday at the Harvest Gala, then. I may be late getting in so I'll just meet you there."

She didn't want to go because there seemed no reason, now, to have to dread the social gathering all week. But she knew if she said so, he'd try to convince her it was important to go, important that she show off her new clothes and the new hairstyle he thought she would have by then. He wanted her to thumb her newly independent nose at the people who had ignored her in the past. Thea knew she could go as bare as Lady Godiva and hardly anyone would notice. She was high society's ugly duckling and nothing was going to make her a swan.

But she couldn't say that to Peter. "Yes," she said as brightly as she could. "I'll see you Saturday."

His smile was nice and she thought if he'd only kiss her goodbye, she could pretend this was just like all the mornings this week when he'd finished his breakfast and left her behind in the apartment. *See you tonight,* he'd say, and she'd close the door and hug the promise close all day until he came back. But the world outside her window was already black with night and morning had long since come and gone.

"I need to go," he said, his absence already hovering like an uninvited guest in the rose and golden room. "Goodbye, Thea."

As the door closed behind him, her fingers dug too deeply into Ally's underbelly and the calico objected with a huffy, *"meow!"* and a spat of claws. Thea pulled her hand back, seeing the blood beading up along her arm, feeling the sting and feeling badly that she'd caused the half-grown kitten any discomfort.

She knew Peter felt badly about having hurt her, too. But she suddenly wished she could have scratched him to let him know that no matter how good his intentions had been, he had hurt her and she did mind. Watching Ally lick her furry stomach and cast accusing glances, Thea thought it must feel good to lick your wounds with a certain *I-didn't-deserve-that* haughtiness, a definite *you-should-be-more-careful* dignity.

Turning from the window seat with sudden purpose, she walked into the dressing room and from there, into the closet. Her clothes—all the new things Peter had bought for her and the few things she had bought for herself—were hung or stacked in spacious nooks, put away with care by unseen hands while she had been at dinner. It was nice, she thought, to have help. At Grace Place, her grandmother had insisted she pick up after herself, create no messes and cause no one any extra work. If anyone had ever hung up her clothes for her before today, Thea certainly didn't recall it.

Running her hands over the blended linens and silks, she felt the luxury of the fabrics, saw the quality of the colors and designs, and wondered why Davinia had never bought her a new dress. Had she been such a troublesome child that she deserved to wear only her mother's ill-fitting leftovers? Had she been just a substitute daughter, a good, biddable Elizabeth, who did whatever she was asked in the hope that she'd be loved for her obedience? Or was she simply the unfortunate child who had been left behind to make amends for all the trouble, all the pain her mother had caused?

But that wasn't fair.

A pool of indignance and anger rippled in the depths of her being and rose in a flood she couldn't stem.

Peter was right. She did deserve better. She could be different. There were some decisions that mattered that were hers, and hers alone, to make. Grabbing the wedding dress, she pulled it off its padded hanger and carried it out to the dressing room, stripping off what she was already wearing as she went. But even before she stepped into the shell pink silk and pulled it up to her breasts, she knew it wasn't the dress that had made the difference. Even with the gown half on, half off, and drooping from her shoulders in loose, corrugated folds, the woman who looked out from the mirror had changed.

She wasn't beautiful. Or pretty. Her hair was a disaster. Her eyes looked wounded and wary.

But there was something resolute about the set of her shoulders, a new determination in the lift of her chin, and the beginning of confidence in the way she stood her ground, giving Thea fair warning that she would not be a wallflower anymore.

"Why, Thea! You've cut your hair." Ilsa Fairchild could hardly believe this was the same young woman. It wasn't just the hair, which was no longer a frazzled, mousey brown, but a sleek fall that framed her face in a gleaming, dark-honey blond. She was wearing makeup. Not much, but enough to add a soft tint to her cheeks, highlight the perfect arch of her brows and emphasize her dark, coffee-brown eyes. Her clothes were stylishly old-fashioned, which suited her, and the colors were a muted blend of autumn pastels. Nothing too vivid, nothing attention-grabbing, and yet, heads turned to watch as Thea passed by. But the change went deeper than appearance. Much deeper.

"Hello, Mrs. Fairchild." Thea smiled shyly and slid into the chair opposite Ilsa at the corner table. "I've never been to The Torrid Tomato. It's a little…noisy, isn't it?"

"It's a lot noisy, but I love the atmosphere, and the artichoke dip appetizer, which I've already ordered for us." Ilsa couldn't stop staring at Thea, couldn't imagine how, in just five days, such a change could have occurred. It was, she thought, a rather strong argument for the existence of fairy godmothers. In particular, one named Ainsley. "I don't want to embarrass you, Thea, but you look gorgeous."

Thea dipped her chin and the gleaming hair swung past her cheeks. "I hardly think *gorgeous* describes me, Mrs. Fairchild," she said. "But thank you for noticing. I'm feeling a little more…confident today."

"I should imagine you are. May I…" Ilsa hesitated. "Is it too gauche to ask if your husband is partly responsible for this…transformation?"

Thea blushed, but her chin came up with an attractive stubbornness. "Peter is responsible," she said. "Even though he doesn't know it."

Hmm. That sounded like the stirring of possibilities. "Oh?" Ilsa said with a diplomatic smile. "I can't believe, Thea, that Peter hasn't noticed the change in you."

"He's in Boston."

"Oh," Ilsa said again, trying to decide what was going on with this couple. The week before they'd been in Boston together. Now Thea was here and Peter was staying in Boston alone. James seemed to think his son had finally realized just what he'd gotten himself into with this marriage. Archer thought Peter simply needed some time to think things through. Ainsley was convinced love was hovering on the horizon. Ilsa was starting to believe all three of them were right. "And you've obviously been keeping yourself busy while he's gone. Ainsley has been bubbling over with excitement this week and being very mysterious about all the shopping trips the two of you have made. Now I can see why.''

''She's been very helpful. We've had quite a time discovering the right style for me. I'm not sure we've hit it yet, but I couldn't have done even this much without her.'' Thea opened her menu, then closed it again, looking self-conscious. ''I never realized how nice it could be to have a friend.''

Ilsa's heart went out to her and she disliked Davinia Carey all the more. ''I'm glad you've discovered that, Thea. Ainsley can't say enough nice things about you.''

The curve of Thea's smile was soft with pleasure. ''I like her very much. She does talk a great deal, though, have you noticed?''

''Once or twice,'' Ilsa said with dry humor. ''She's certainly enlivened the office since she started working with me.''

''She idolizes you, Mrs. Fairchild.''

''Please, call me Ilsa.''

''Ilsa.'' Thea complied with obvious delight. ''Ainsley says she doesn't think you'll be Mrs. Fairchild much longer, anyway.''

''As we just agreed, Ainsley talks a great deal and sometimes about things that really are not her business.''

Thea flushed. ''I guess I shouldn't have told you, but I'm so...pleased for you. I like Mr. Braddock.'' She paused. ''Mr. *James* Braddock. He's been very nice to me while I've been staying at the Hall. Well, they've all been nice. Mr. Archer, too. And Abbott and Ruth. Bryce and Lara stay mostly in town or at their place in Watch Hill, but they've gone out of their way to make sure I've felt welcome at Braddock Hall. I haven't talked to the chauffeur much because I've been driving myself all over the place.''

"Good for you, Thea.'' Ilsa was delighted to see Thea finally coming into her own. ''Peter must be so proud of you.''

Thea's expression changed then, reverted for a moment to the awkward, unassertive girl she used to be. ''That's why I asked you to meet me for lunch. I...wanted to talk to you about Peter, Mrs. Fairchild. Ilsa.'' She ran her finger down the edge of the menu, seeming to gather courage simply by taking her time. ''Please don't be upset, but I know you're a...a matchmaker. And please don't be mad at Ainsley because I knew even before she let it slip.''

Ilsa made a mental note to have the *discretion-is-crucial* talk with her apprentice one more time, even as she smiled encouragingly. ''It's not a state secret, Thea. I just try not to advertise it.''

Thea nodded. ''I heard rumors a long time ago. It's kind of funny, but at social events, people seem to forget I'm around and they'll sometimes have the most private conversations where I can't help but overhear. That's how I knew you made a match for Christina Conrad a couple of years ago and for Patrick Simons just last year. I also heard that you set up the match for Angela Merchant when Peter broke up with her.

And I know…well, I *think* you had a hand in both Adam's and Bryce's recent matches.''

It was Ilsa's policy never to acknowledge or deny that sort of information, so she simply smiled and waited for Thea to continue.

"And well, it seemed to me that if you'd done that, you might have, probably *had,* chosen someone for…for Peter and it all got messed up when he took me to Angela's wedding and…'' Thea's voice faded from soft to too soft to hear, but then came back with a poignant, "and I wanted you to know how sorry I am for getting Peter all mixed up in my problems and maybe…costing him a chance with the woman you'd chosen as his…his perfect match.''

Ilsa debated for perhaps half a second before she broke one of her own, cardinal rules. "I'm the one who should apologize to you for setting up that fateful date in the first place.'' She saw Thea frown in confusion and decided Ainsley hadn't confessed the whole, so perhaps her apprentice had some sense of discretion, after all. "Angela's wedding was supposed to be the *introduction of possibilities* for the two of you.''

"The two of…us?'' Thea asked, still mystified or simply unwilling to believe.

"Thea,'' Ilsa said gently. "*You* are the woman I matched with Peter.''

With a startled blink, Thea opened her mouth, then closed it again. She reached for the glass of water on the table in front of her and took a long drink. "Why would you do that?'' she asked finally.

"I deal in possibilities, Thea. I look for connections others miss. I saw both when I saw you and Peter together. Whether you were dancing or just talking, there was something there between the two of you. My intuition, which is my stock in trade, told me it was worth pursuing. So with Archer's help, I set up that first date to Angela's wedding. I can't explain it any better than that I felt there were possibilities between you two. It was a feeling I had then, a feeling I still have now."

Setting the glass of water back on the table, Thea gave a tremulous sigh. "Thank you," she said, looking up. "I can't imagine how you came to think I might...that Peter would..." She met Ilsa's gaze. "But it means a lot to me that you did." She pulled at her lower lip with her teeth, as if she were searching for words, trying to find the right ones. "I'm going to get an annulment," she said. "I talked with the attorney about that yesterday."

Ilsa's heart sank, but she managed only a concerned little arching of her eyebrows. "An annulment?"

"I think it's best. There was no need for us to get married in the first place except that I would never have had the courage to stand up to my grandmother if Peter hadn't forced the issue. And please don't misunderstand. I know this marriage was the best thing that ever could have happened to me and I'll always be grateful to Peter for making such a sacrifice, but it's not...not a real marriage and the sooner I'm out of his life, the sooner he can find the right woman. The sooner maybe you can make the right match for him."

"What about you, Thea? Is there a right match for you?"

The tight curve of her lips held for a moment, then resolved into a brave and genuine smile. "You probably already know the answer to that, but please don't worry about me. I've already had more happiness than I thought was possible, more than some people ever find. I'm going to be okay."

Ilsa studied this new Thea for a moment. "I'm proud of you, Thea Braddock," she said. "Enormously proud."

"Berenson," Thea corrected, taking no claim to Peter's name. "And, thank you, Ilsa. I'm beginning to feel a little proud of myself."

And if that was the only thing to have come from this match that had seemed so improbable at the start, then Ilsa could feel she'd done a good thing by following her intuition. But she wasn't yet convinced the possibilities had run their course. *It isn't over until the wedding bells ring,* Ainsley liked to say. Ilsa knew, however, that the wedding bells were only the beginning of the love affair. "Are you and Peter going to the Harvest Gala tomorrow night?" she asked innocently, as if Ainsley hadn't already told her they were.

"Not together." Thea moved her glass aside as the waiter brought their appetizer and placed it on the table. "Peter said he'd be there, but…" Her voice trailed off into doubt. "I wish I wasn't going. I've been dreading it all week because Grandmother always attends and because…well, it'll be the first time I'm going with the intention of *not* being a wallflower. I don't know which one scares me more. But I've decided to stop hiding and be brave, even if nobody notices. And tomorrow night is as good a time to start as any.''

"Bravo, Thea." Ilsa hoped Thea would quickly discover she'd already faced the toughest part in simply making the decision to change. This confident young woman, who was emerging from the ashes of her shyness and self-denial, was going to cause quite a stir wherever she went from now on. "I was just thinking...there's a vacancy on the library board. Would you be interested?"

Thea couldn't quite disguise her reaction, a mixture of devout apprehension and tempered excitement. "Do you think they'd want *me?*"

"I think they'd be lucky to get you. And now, would you please take some of the artichoke dip? Once I get started on it, the stuff has a way of mysteriously disappearing and you may not get another chance."

Thea laughed and reached for the appetizer.

THE WHOLE OFFICE overflowed with laughter and good wishes.

"Congratulations, Peter!"

"The Pierce Award. Wow, Peter, what an honor."

"You deserve it. The Atlanta Complex is the best piece of architecture this firm has ever turned out."

"*This* firm? It's the best piece any of us are ever likely to see in our careers."

"At least until Peter turns in the Boston project."

And the congratulatory laughter made the rounds all over again. The accolades from his associates had been growing grander in scale ever since Vic Luttrell had taken the call notifying the firm that Peter had won the prestigious Pierce Award. Champagne had appeared and suit coats had been taken off, leaving a lot of shirt sleeves and loosened ties as the party revved up. Peter vacillated between bursts of elation and a bone weary sadness. He drank the champagne and accepted the congratulations, withstood the handshakes and the hefty pats on the back, fielded phone calls and laughed at every joke.

But for all his genuine happiness at winning the Pierce, he couldn't get past the knowledge that something was missing from his celebration.

His grandfather had called.

James, Adam and Bryce had phoned in their congratulations, too, and both of his sisters-in-law had gushed over his success.

His co-workers were thrilled for him and having a great time at this impromptu party.

Some of his friends in Boston had dropped by with their good wishes.

Plans were already afoot in Sea Change for another party to celebrate his victory.

There was no reason he shouldn't be having the time of his life.

Except for Thea.

The memory of her face as he'd left her on Sunday night had haunted him all week. The knowledge that he'd hurt her nagged at him like a festering splinter. He hadn't called or talked to her since, because he thought that would only make a complicated situation worse. He hadn't meant for her to fall in love with him. He'd never intended for her to think this marriage was anything other than a temporary arrangement. He hadn't expected her to bring so much trust and faith and hope into the relationship. Now, of course, he couldn't understand why he hadn't foreseen those possibilities. She'd never had a champion, never known the simple courtesies most women took for granted. It was only natural she'd read something into his actions which wasn't there.

Someone clapped him on the shoulder and as he turned to accept another handshake, another *good job,* he saw the sketch of his stepfather and knew what a lie all of his justifications were.

He'd made love to her...and often. He'd shared his bed with her at night and eaten the breakfast she fixed for him in the morning. He'd kissed her hello and goodbye, just for the pleasure of it. He'd taken her hand in his, put his coat across her shoulders when she was cold, and he'd called her sometimes from the office just to see what she was doing. He'd looked forward to the end of the day when he could go home to her and he'd savored the way her dark eyes lit up at the sight of him. He'd felt protective and tender and loving.

So how had he not realized he was falling in love with her?

In the midst of the gaiety all around him, Peter remembered her in his office, touching the desk lightly so as not to leave a mark, admiring the sketches he'd made to remind him of his roots, telling him that art was emotion on paper.

"Congratulations, Peter!"

"Yeah, man, way to go."

Another pat on the back, another good-natured handshake, another toast of champagne. And all of it meant nothing because a little wallflower of a woman wasn't there to share it with him.

How had she settled into his heart without his knowledge or permission? How was it possible he could have fallen in love with a woman who was so *not* what he'd always believed he wanted? She wasn't blond or beautiful or one of high society's reigning belles. She didn't know how to flirt or play the parlor games of seduction. She had none of the graceful social skills of her class, although she was always, unquestionably a lady. She wasn't at all the kind of woman he had wanted for his wife.

So how had she turned out to be the wife he wanted?

He lifted the phone to call her, to tell her he was coming home now to Braddock Hall, to her, but someone popped the cork on another bottle of champagne, someone else called for another toast, and he replaced the receiver. Thea deserved better than a long distance *I love you,* shouted over a hubbub of strange voices. She deserved flowers and romance and a ring. She deserved a proper proposal and the soft, slow courtship of words. She deserved a better husband than he could ever be.

But he must be the luckiest man alive, because he was pretty certain she thought he was the husband she should have.

Chapter Eleven

For someone who normally steered clear of mirrors, Thea had spent an inordinate amount of time in front of one lately. She couldn't get over the change in her appearance, couldn't stop touching her hair or being amazed by the way the right makeup made her eyes look large and luminous and lent a healthy glow to her skin. She'd tried makeup before, hiding out in her room with her contraband Cover Girl cosmetics and a *Glamour* magazine, but with no one to show her how, no one to say, *try this color, do it this way, or that looks good,* her efforts had been worse than dismal. Sadie had tried to help her a few times, but Davinia had had a fit when she saw the blue eye shadow on her twelve-year-old granddaughter and poor Sadie and Monroe very nearly got fired over the incident. After that, Thea didn't dare ask anyone else for advice on how to be a girl.

And to be honest, when she and Ainsley had started out on the quest for a make-over, Thea hadn't believed the right clothes, the right makeup or a new hairstyle would make a difference. She'd expected, at best, to look less like a misfit, more like a well-dressed wall-flower. But with every day, she'd gained a little more confidence, a bit more knowledge of what she liked and what suited her. For years, she'd watched from the sidelines and recognized that attractive women were confident, but until now, she hadn't realized that the confidence came first and was, in essence, the attraction.

And that is what she saw now in her own reflection. The confident woman who looked back at her wasn't beautiful. Her face would never launch a skiff, much less a thousand ships. But Thea didn't want perfection. She only wanted to cause a small stir at the Harvest Gala tonight. And she thought, perhaps, she just might look good enough to do that.

The dress she'd chosen with Ainsley's help was simply made with a cowl collar, a low, squared off back, and a soft bell shaped skirt that curved out over her hips from a waist so small Thea could hardly believe it was hers. The fabric was silk, although it had the look of linen, and the color was such a pretty shade of leaf green she couldn't stop touching it. She regretted now not buying the nice set of costume jewelry Ainsley had suggested. But since she was spending Peter's money until she had access to her trust—which the attorney had said could take months—she didn't want to spend too freely. She already owed him more than money could ever repay, and she didn't mean to be too deeply in his debt. Still, the earrings would have been a nice touch.

With a cautioning lift of her eyebrow, Thea reminded herself this was merely her first foray into society as a brave woman. There would be other occasions for jewelry, other times when she would feel confident enough to wear diamonds. For tonight, she was the best she could be, and she hoped with all her heart that when Peter saw her, he would be proud of her, too. Picking up the alpaca shawl, she draped it across her arm and headed downstairs.

Archer Braddock was awaiting her in the foyer, standing at the foot of the stairs, talking softly with Abbott, who held Archer's black coat, hat and cherrywood cane. The murmur of their voices brought a flurry of trepidation rising in Thea's throat. The last time she'd come down these stairs and met Archer at the bottom, had been her wedding to Peter. She wasn't as scared this time, but she was plenty nervous. Taking a deep breath, she made up her mind that tonight she wouldn't faint. No matter what happened, she would not faint.

As she took the next step, her gown made a whispery, silky rustle and the men glanced up. Thea held her breath, not knowing what to expect, but then she saw the curve of their smiles and decided maybe she looked all right, after all.

"Hello," she said when they only stood there, watching her descent. "Have I kept you waiting?"

"As my Janey would say, keeping a man waiting is

a lady's prerogative and a gentleman's privilege.'' Archer offered her a hand down from the last step and held it for a moment, admiring her. "You look lovely, Thea. In fact, you quite remind me of my Jane."

Thea thought that was a sweet thing to say, but unnecessarily flattering. "Thank you, Mr. Braddock, but I remember her and she was very beautiful."

Archer's smile was gently truthful. "Yes, she was, which must be one of the reasons I think of her every time I look at you."

She was no match for these Braddock men, Thea thought. She might as well not even try to be. So she smiled and accepted the compliment as graciously as she knew he'd meant it. "Thank you. I think I'm ready to go."

"In a moment." Archer extended his other hand to her and in his palm was a small, black jeweler's box. "It would please me very much if you would wear these tonight, Thea."

The box held a pair of pearl and diamond earrings, breathtaking in their simplicity, delicately beautiful in their design. She couldn't help but reach to touch them, even though she knew she could never do them justice. "Oh," she said. "They're so pretty."

"They were Jane's. I know she would want you to have them."

"Have them?" Thea couldn't believe he would give her such a gift. "Oh, but I couldn't..."

"You're a part of this family, Thea. Consider these a belated wedding gift from Jane and from me."

She wasn't really a Braddock, had no right to accept such a wonderful gift, but beneath her fingertip, the earrings felt cool and tempting. "Thank you, Mr. Braddock, but I don't think Peter would…"

Archer put the box into her palm and patted her hand. "Put them on. Wear them with grace and pleasure, because they belonged to Peter's grandmother and because you are Peter's wife."

And so she was. If only for a few more nights.

Blinking back tears, she handed Abbott her shawl and walked to one of the large, gilt mirrors that adorned the entrance hall. There, she leaned in and put on Jane Braddock's earrings.

"And now," Archer said approvingly when she returned to the foot of the stairs. "Perhaps we should go. We wouldn't want to arrive late at the Harvest ball."

PETER WAS LATE leaving Boston because he'd had to visit three different jewelers before he found the ring he wanted. Even then, he'd had to wait for the setting to be cleaned and checked and for the ring to be sized. He'd known in a glance it would be too large and he wanted it to be perfect. Or as perfect as he could make it. He'd planned to be at the Hall before Thea left for the gala, but he'd missed her departure by twenty minutes. So he slowed down, took a shower and changed into his tux, thinking ahead, imagining how she'd look when he told her he loved her, smiling as he envisioned what she'd say when he gave her the ring.

He recognized a nervous ache in his stomach as he walked through the doors of The Breakers and into the opulent summer-home world of the Vanderbilt's. It was decorated for an autumn harvest, although the mansion needed no embellishment and, as if the reds and golds of the huge open great room weren't enough, color flashed from the walkways above as guests meandered, in their sparkling best, through the upstairs halls. Peter said "hello" and "how are you" to people he knew as he searched for Thea, hoping to see her in one of her usual haunts, along the perimeters of the crowd or in a corner of the room.

But, in truth, he walked right past her before he heard her voice and realized the woman in the center of a vivacious group was his wife.

"Peter?" she said. "My, aren't you fashionably late."

He was struck momentarily dumb with astonishment as he turned for a second look. "Thea?" he said hoarsely and not at all the way he'd meant. She was different. Her hair was blond—*blond*—and no longer drooping in its usual ragtag fashion, but pulled back from her face and curling softly, fashionably behind her ears and along her nape. Her dress was form-fitting and flattering and looked so good on her it made his heart race. She was wearing makeup and his grandmother's pearl and diamond earrings. Her smile was welcoming, but held none of the shy, innocent pleasure he'd become accustomed to seeing when she smiled at him. But the difference wasn't all in appearance. It was in the tilt of her head, in the wary look in her eyes, in the way her gaze never flickered from his. As if she expected something from him, and wasn't seeing it. As if she had realized what she deserved and knew he could never give it to her.

His nervous stomach twisted in panic. He had to say what he'd come to say before he lost all sense of time and place and just kissed her. Here and now, with all the love and desire boiling inside him...which was not at all the sort of thing a gentleman did to a lady at the Harvest Gala. "I have to talk to you. Now. Alone." He reached for her arm, but with a single lift of her brow, she stopped him and turned, with a soft smile, to the group of friends he hadn't even yet acknowledged. "Excuse us, please," she said, and then turning, she walked away and Peter didn't know what else to do but fall into step beside her.

"Thea! You look marvelous!"

"Beautiful dress, Thea."

"You must tell me who did your hair, Thea."

She was greeted along the way like an old friend, as if these people hadn't ignored her in the past, as if now that she'd changed the way she looked, all was forgotten. It bothered him for her, but she didn't seem to mind. She acknowledged each compliment, blushed a little with the attention, and kept moving steadily through the crowd toward the entrance and the portico beyond. The wind was cold coming off the ocean, and she shivered slightly as she moved along the front of the house, away from the lights and the limousines and the dwindling stream of disembarking guests.

When she turned to him, his heart squeezed painfully tight in his chest because he loved her so much.

"What is it, Peter?" Her chin came up with the words and she was breathing fast, as if she expected a fight. "I can see you're upset by the...the way I look."

"You look beautiful," he said and meant it. "I can't believe you've changed so much. I never thought you would look so...different." He wanted to kiss her so badly, but first he had to tell her what he'd been waiting a lifetime to say. "I...Thea, I love you."

Her expression changed, went from apprehensive to bewildered and then slowly settled into a cool mask of comprehension. "Don't do this, Peter. Not tonight. Or ever. I didn't need your pity before and I don't need this...this sudden change of heart now that you think I look halfway presentable. All I wanted was for you to be proud of me tonight. I know you don't love me. I never expected that you would." Her eyes shone with unshed tears, but she kept her chin up and faced down the protests sputtering on his lips. "But you can't treat me like some...some noble experiment. I won't let you."

He was both awed and alarmed by her fierceness, equally admiring of and angered by her declaration. "I never meant to hurt you, Thea, and I certainly never considered you an experiment."

"Didn't you, Peter? Didn't you marry me to prove to yourself you could be a hero? A champion of misfits?'' She ran out of steam then, and the tears threatened to spill, but with more poise than he'd ever imagined she would have, she blinked them back. ''Look, I don't want to talk about this. I appreciate what you did for me, Peter. I do. But I don't want you to feel you're responsible for me, so I called Chip yesterday and told him to file the annulment papers as soon as possible. You'll need to sign them, but that's mostly a formality. It should be done in a few days.''

''Thea,'' he said, feeling suddenly desperate. ''I don't want an annulment.''

Her sigh was deep and resolute. ''It's better this way, Peter. I'll deal with Grandmother and the trust. You have given me the confidence I needed to make my own decisions. I can never repay you for that but, for what it's worth, thank you.''

She stepped around him, moving in a warning rustle of silk, leaving him angry and bewildered and frustrated. He should stop her, but he'd already said he loved her and for the life of him, he couldn't think of another thing to say.

''Oh, and Peter?'' He heard her stop and waited, hoping she had changed her mind, hoping she felt his heart reaching out to her, hoping so hard it was a physical pain. ''Congratulations on winning the Pierce Award. You deserve the best.''

Then she was gone, disappearing into the lights and the noise of the party within, leaving him outside alone in the cold, sea-scented wind.

It didn't take five minutes before he went after her.

"THEA?" Davinia's voice caught her before she could make it into the lady's room and privacy. "I will have a word with you now, Thea."

Thea dropped her hand from the doorknob, and told herself this was a public place with people all around. Her grandmother wouldn't make a scene. Not here. Gathering her courage all over again, she turned and came face to face with her grandmother and all the things, both bad and good, that had made up her life before Peter came to her rescue. "Hello, Grandmother," she said. "You look very nice."

Coolly critical, Davinia's eyes raked her from head to foot. "You look like…Elizabeth."

It didn't sound like a compliment, but Thea chose to consider it one. "Thank you," she said.

"That was not a compliment."

Davinia's frown had always struck Thea with acute agony, but amazingly, she discovered that when met with a lift of her own newly stubborn chin, her grandmother's disapproval lost some of its edge. "I'm sorry you feel that way, Grandmother, because I like the way I look. And I have no intention of going back to the way I was before."

Davinia sniffed. "I wish for you to return home, Theadosia."

That sounded like a command, but Thea chose to believe it wasn't. "I'm sorry, but I don't think I can do that."

"You can and you will, because Grace Place is your home."

She didn't have a home. She didn't belong at Grace Place anymore and she'd never belonged at Braddock Hall. But someday soon she'd have a place of her own. A home with flowering shrubs and bright paint and a welcome mat. A home where she and her cats could be happy. "I will come and visit you, Grandmother," she said. "We need to discuss a great many things."

"I suppose you want money. That's all Elizabeth wanted from me, too. But I won't bend on this, Thea."

The very fact that Davinia Grace Carey would mention money in a public setting was proof she was very upset. Thea felt sorry for her, but she knew she had to stand strong now or forever let her grandmother browbeat her into silence. She clenched her hands to keep them from shaking. *Be brave,* she told herself. *Be brave.* "I want what is rightfully mine," she said. "I also want to have a relationship with you. I don't believe I should have to give up one for the other."

"You have obviously made that choice already."

"No, but I will if you force me. Don't do that, Grandmother. Please, don't do that."

"I imagine it's that Braddock boy who has put you up to this. I did warn you he couldn't make you happy, Thea. He married you to get you away from me and to lay some legitimate claim to the blue blood of the upper classes. You can't believe it was a love match. Or ever could be."

"You're wrong about that, Mrs. Carey." Peter spoke from behind Davinia and Thea's heart skipped a beat and then another. Her mouth went dry and she reached behind her for the doorknob because she needed to hold on to something as her grandmother flushed with anger and Peter's eyes sought Thea's with a look so tender, so honest, she thought it must be the truth. "Thea and I are a love match. And it has nothing to do with who our mothers were, or who anyone else thinks we are, or taking her away from you, or how she looks tonight, or any other reason except that I love your granddaughter with every breath I take. I love the way she smiles first thing in the morning and I love the way she drinks her orange juice. I love the way she pours her heart into her sketches and I love the way she loves her cats. I love that she dances when she's happy and I love it when she wears my shirts. I am proud of the man I am when I am with her and I am proud of the woman she is becoming. I will love her to the day I die and, if she can love me at all, I swear I will spend the rest of my life making her happy."

Thea was afraid the rest of her life might not last very long because she couldn't breathe at all and her heart was racing and her palms were sweaty. But from somewhere in the depths of her newfound confidence, she managed a soft, wondrous whisper. "I love you, Peter. I do love you."

"I'm glad," he said. "Because I love you so much it hurts."

It was the last thing she heard before she fainted.

Epilogue

Archer looked around the dining table, past the Thanksgiving Day cornucopia, the turkey and the trimmings,
to the family gathered on this holiday at Braddock Hall.
Katie and Adam to his right, Ilsa and James next, then
across from them at the table were Bryce and Lara,
then Peter and Thea to Archer's left. At the opposite
end, on a pillow to give him height in the chair, sat
Calvin, all gap-toothed smile at being invited to sit with
the grown-ups.

The conversation was a mix of plans: Adam and Katie's plans to move back to the Hall before Christmas
and begin setting up their nursery; Bryce and Lara's—
and Cal's—plans to sail to Florida and visit Disney
World; Peter and Thea's plans to build a house near
Boston with lots of windows, a colorful array of shrubs
and a room especially for the cats; Adam's plans to
rejoin Braddock Industries as CEO after the first of the
year; Katie's plans to renovate an old building in Sea
Change and open a tea room, along with taking a seat
on the town council; Bryce's plans to head up the new

Braddock Family Foundation; Lara's plans to help her
sisters complete their educations; Peter's plans for the
design of the new house; Thea's plans to open an art
school for underprivileged children; Calvin's plans to
meet Mickey Mouse; James and Ilsa's as yet unofficial
plans for a wedding.

Another wedding.

Archer was hoping they'd marry at Christmas and
give the family four weddings in less than twelve
months, which would be a fitting end to a quite extraordinary year for the Braddock family. It was also
quite fitting, Archer thought, that the extraordinary
matchmaker of IF Enterprises had met her match in a
Braddock man. And James, at last, had found in Ilsa
the love he had sought for so long.

It was a good day to be thankful.

"A toast." James rose, as did each one of his sons,
raising their glasses. "To the ladies of Braddock Hall.
Katie, Lara, Thea and Ilsa. What took you so long?"

Everyone laughed and then Katie lifted her glass of
grape juice with a teasing smile. "We couldn't get you
Braddock men to listen!"

"Or be serious!" Lara joined in.

"Or realize what you'd found," Thea said, blushing
with the newness of being loved.

"Or maybe," Ilsa said with a small, secret smile,
"we just wanted you to see the possibilities for your-
selves."

Calvin, not wanting to be left out, grabbed his Donald Duck cup and stood up on the pillow. "Rub-a-dub-dub. Thanks for the grub. Yea, God. Let's eat!"

The laughter went around the table again, comforting Archer with its warmth and ready affection. One for all. All for one. He couldn't have been more proud of the family he and Jane had made...with just a little help from Ilsa.

As Calvin's parents got him settled back in his seat, cautioning him gently about remembering his manners, Adam leaned over to whisper in Katie's ear, James made a private toast with Ilsa and Peter kissed Thea, his bride.

Archer smiled and got a bit misty-eyed with gratitude. *Ah, Janey. Look what our love has created, look at the legacy we're leaving behind.*

And even before the Thanksgiving prayer was begun, he was certain he felt the brush of her angel kiss on his cheek.

It was, indeed, a good day for thanksgiving.

Coming in April 2002
from

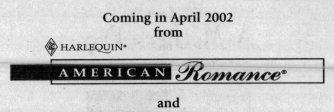

HARLEQUIN®

AMERICAN *Romance*®

and

Judy
Christenberry

RANDALL RICHES
(HAR #918)

Desperate to return to his Wyoming ranch, champion bull
rider Rich Randall had no choice but to accept sassy
Samantha Jeffer's helping hand—with a strict
"no hanky-panky" warning. But on the long road home
something changed and Rich was suddenly thinking of
turning in his infamous playboy status
for a little band of gold.

Don't miss this heartwarming addition to the series,

Brides
for Brothers

Available wherever Harlequin books are sold.

HARLEQUIN®
Makes any time special®

Visit us at www.eHarlequin.com

HARRR

Every day is

A Mother's Day

in this heartwarming anthology
celebrating motherhood and romance!

Featuring the classic story "Nobody's Child" by Emilie Richards
He had come to a child's rescue, and now Officer Farrell Riley was
suddenly sharing parenthood with beautiful Gemma Hancock.
But would their ready-made family last forever?

Plus two brand-new romances:

"Baby on the Way" by Marie Ferrarella
Single and pregnant, Madeline Reed found the perfect husband in the
handsome cop who helped bring her infant son into the world. But did his
dutiful role in the surprise delivery make J. T. Walker a daddy?

"A Daddy for Her Daughters" by Elizabeth Bevarly
When confronted with spirited Naomi Carmichael and her brood of girls,
bachelor Sloan Sullivan realized he had a lot to learn about women!
Especially if he hoped to win this sexy single mom's heart…

Available this April from Silhouette Books!

Where love comes alive™

TRUEBLOOD, TEXAS

Coming in May 2002...

RODEO DADDY

by

B.J. Daniels

Lost:

Her first and only love.
Chelsea Jensen discovers
ten years later that her father
had been to blame for
Jack Shane's disappearance
from her family's ranch.

Found:

A canceled check. Now Chelsea
knows why Jack left her. Had he ever loved her, or had she
been too young and too blind to see the truth?

**Chelsea is determined to track Jack down and find out.
And what a surprise she gets when she finds him!**

Finders Keepers: bringing families together

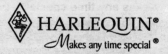